BLACK HARVEST

NIGEL GRAY
(Adapted from the novel by Ann Pilling)

Additional Material
Jan Dean

Series Consultant
Cecily O'Neill

CollinsEducational
An imprint of HarperCollins*Publishers*

Copyright © 1986 Nigel Gray

www.CollinsEducation.com

On-line support for schools and colleges

First published 1986

20 19 18 17 16

ISBN-13 978-0-00-330233-2

ISBN-10 0-00-330233-4

Acknowledgements
The authors and publishers would like to thank the following for permission
to reproduce copyright material:
The Times, pages 68–69; Thomas Nelson, page 74; Robert Hale, page 75;
Macmillan, page 76; Edward Arnold, pages 77–78; Pergamon Press, pages
78–79; William Collins, page 80; William Heinemann, pages 82–86;
Graham Turner, *Sunday Telegraph*, page 88; *The Guardian*, page 88; Oxfam,
pages 89–91.

Photographs
Illustrated London News, pages 66, 68, 71, 72; The Bettmann Archive, BBC
Hutton Picture Library, pages 83, 85.

Design by The Pinpoint Design Company

Typeset by Hope Services, Abingdon.

Printed and bound in China by Imago

CONTENTS

The Characters

COLIN   A bright boy of thirteen, more interested in sports and outdoor activities than studying or reading.

PRILL   Colin's eleven-year-old sister — rather more sensitive than her brother.

OLIVER   Their nine-year-old cousin. A quiet, pedantic, intelligent and studious boy from an old-fashioned home, who tends to irritate Colin.

MUM   Colin and Prill's mother — the sort of parent who allows her children plenty of freedom and expects responsibility in return.

DAD   Their father — also a sensible and tolerant parent.

FATHER HAGAN   A priest, more than averagely conscientious, tolerant and benign.

DONAL   An old man who lives alone with bitter and painful memories.

MRS O'MALLEY   A farmer's wife — friendly, kind and generous.

KEVIN   Her sixteen-year-old son, who has inherited his mother's good nature.

DR DONOVAN   Old, irritable, surly and brusque, and, 'on the bottle'.

The setting is a beautiful bay on the west coast of Ireland: a newly-built holiday bungalow set in farmland with a view of the sea. Nearby is the O'Malley farmhouse, and old Donal's caravan. The farm is a few kilometres from the village of Ballimagliesh.

BLACK HARVEST

Day One
SCENE ONE

Prill's *bedroom. Day.* **Colin** *is sitting on the edge of* **Prill's** *bed while* **Prill** *is unpacking her clothes.*

COLIN   I thought we were never going to get here.

PRILL   Me too.

COLIN   That weed, Oliver! What did we have to cart him along for?

PRILL   I suppose he can't help it. It's the first time he's ever been away from his mum.

COLIN   Why couldn't we have had some decent cousins? I hate kids who keep being car sick. It's bad enough with the baby and everything.

PRILL   But it's nice here — now we've actually arrived.

COLIN   Yeah. Smashing.

PRILL   Except I was expecting an old house. Not everything brand new like this.

COLIN   Dad's friend's never even been here yet. We're the first people to stay in it.

PRILL   It's a bit posh though. Mum's scared Alison's going to make a mess on the carpet.

COLIN   Well, it's a stupid colour, cream, for a carpet you've got to walk on. And it's not fair having to keep Jessie chained up outside.

PRILL   But I think she'll love it here — running on the beach and everything. And my room's lovely.

COLIN   Yeah. **You** don't have to share a room with that creep, Oliver.

1

PRILL Where is he now?

COLIN He's got his nose stuck in a book about insects or something.

PRILL Already?

COLIN He was reading about Irish history in the car.

PRILL I know.

COLIN And this is supposed to be a holiday!

PRILL Whew! I'm so hot. I thought it was always raining in Ireland.

COLIN I'll open the window.

PRILL I've tried. It's all stuck with the new paint.

Colin *and* **Prill** *cross to the window.* **Colin** *tries to open it and fails. He bangs with his fist all around the frame.*

PRILL Careful!

Another few bangs and the window shudders open. **Colin** *and* **Prill** *lean on the sill, looking out.*

PRILL I wonder why he made such a wide drive?

COLIN So he could swing his car round in front of the house. He's probably got a Rolls Royce if he can afford to build all this.

PRILL Or so the removal lorry could turn round and things like that.

COLIN I wonder what's behind those trees.

PRILL Fields I suppose.

COLIN Cor! Look at the sea.

By leaning well out and looking to the side they can see the bay.

PRILL It's beautiful here.

COLIN I hope Mum remembered to pack my goggles and flippers.

PRILL You should pack your own things.

COLIN Don't you start! Goody Two-Shoes!

PRILL I wish Dad didn't have to go to Dublin.

COLIN Me too. But it's only for the first week.

SCENE TWO

Kitchen. Day. **Mum, Dad, Colin, Prill** *and* **Oliver** *are drinking tea or lemonade and eating biscuits with* **Father Hagan.**

FATHER HAGAN Well, you have a fine family, Mrs Blakeman.

MUM Oh, thank you. In fact only the two eldest are ours. Oliver is my sister's son.

OLIVER By adoption.

MUM Well, yes.

FATHER HAGAN Ah, that explains the differences — in build and colouring, I mean.

DAD And we have a baby girl.

MUM Alison. She's sleeping.

FATHER HAGAN Oh, good, good. A grand family. They'll surely see to your comfort when you're old and grey.

DAD We hope so.

MUM The baby's not too well, actually.

FATHER HAGAN I'm sorry to hear that.

DAD Nothing serious.

MUM Just since we arrived, really.

FATHER HAGAN Please God she'll soon be better.

DAD I think it's just the journey. She'll be as right as rain tomorrow.

FATHER HAGAN I'm sure she will.

MUM I don't know why I mentioned it.

FATHER HAGAN A mother wouldn't be a mother if she didn't worry about her little ones.

PRILL I'm going for a walk along the beach, Mum. Shall I take Alison with me?

MUM I shouldn't disturb her if she's asleep.

DAD Oh, let her take her. The fresh air will do her good. Put her in the sling, Prill.

PRILL *to the boys* Do you two want to come?

COLIN No. I'm going swimming.

OLIVER I think I'll stay and read, thank you.

Colin *and* **Prill** *exchange looks.*

DAD Run along then. We'll have supper in about an hour.

MUM And be careful, Colin.

Colin, Prill *and* **Oliver** *exit.*

FATHER HAGAN I suppose you won't have met old Donal yet — Donal Morrissey?

DAD We've not really finished unpacking.

MUM We talked to Mrs O'Malley of course, up at the farm.

FATHER HAGAN Of course. A grand lady.

MUM Yes. She was so friendly and welcoming.

FATHER HAGAN Donal might be less so. Sure, he's a good soul right enough. But he's got to that stage of life when the smallest change upsets him. He must be getting on for ninety now.

DAD Does he live nearby?

FATHER HAGAN He does. You can see the smoke from his stove rising above the trees, look. He's lived in an old caravan there for years and worked on the O'Malley farm since he was a young man. He got very disturbed when they began building this bungalow. He didn't like the noise and the lorries going up and down the track.

MUM It must have been very quiet before.

FATHER HAGAN It was that.

DAD I'm surprised the O'Malleys sold the land.

FATHER HAGAN Well, it's the usual story with small farmers. They've had a run of poor harvests and were in debt and needed the money.

DAD Well their bad fortune was certainly my colleague's good luck.

FATHER HAGAN That's the way of the world, so it is. *He begins to get up from the table* Well, I must be on my way. I just wanted to wish you all a good holiday. Ballimagliesh is my parish. My house is the last on the road as you leave the village, next to Mooney's Store. Just knock on my door if I can be of any help.

Dad *and* **Mum** *get up and accompany him to the door.*

MUM That's very kind of you.

DAD   Thank you for calling.

FATHER HAGAN   And thank you for the tea.

MUM   Come again, if you're down this way.

FATHER HAGAN   Thank you, thank you. Goodbye for now.

DAD   Goodbye.

MUM   Goodbye.

Day Two
SCENE THREE

Kitchen. Day. **Mum** *and* **Prill** *are cleaning up. In the background we hear the sounds of someone digging.*

PRILL   I wish Dad hadn't gone.

MUM   I know, dear. But if he didn't work we wouldn't be able to afford to go on holiday at all.

PRILL   I'd rather stay at home with him than go on holiday without him.

MUM   He had to come to Ireland anyway, and his friend offered us the use of this house — whatever's the matter with you? Think of all the children who'd love to be able to go on holiday to somewhere like this.

PRILL   I know. I've just got a funny feeling about this place, that's all.

The **Baby** *begins to cry in the bedroom.*

MUM   Stop moping around, for heaven's sake. Take yourself out for a walk. Oh, listen. Alison's crying again.

Mum *leaves the kitchen as* **Colin** *enters from outside looking hot and bothered.*

COLIN   That blasted dog's run off somewhere.

PRILL   I thought she was chained up.

COLIN   She was — but she got free. I can't find her and I've looked all over the place.

PRILL   She'll come back when she's hungry.

COLIN   I'm going down the beach to cool off. You coming?

PRILL   I don't know.

COLIN   What's the matter with you? You've been hanging

about the house all day. You haven't been in the sea once yet.

PRILL I know.

COLIN Well?

PRILL *she looks towards the bedroom where the* **Baby** *is still crying, and lowers her voice* You know when I went for a walk yesterday, when we first got here — it was really horrible. It was so hot and quiet, and there was this terrible smell.

COLIN What sort of smell? I didn't smell anything.

PRILL It was further along from where you were. It was a sort of rotten, sweet smell.

COLIN Was it like pigs?

PRILL No.

COLIN *grinning* Remember that time we went on holiday to that farmhouse, and it was a **pig** farm?

PRILL Yes. But it wasn't anything like that.

COLIN The farmers have probably been muck-spreading, that's all.

PRILL No. It was worse than that. I thought there might be a rotting sheep or a dead dog or something, but I couldn't see anything.

COLIN Probably rotten seaweed. That smells horrible sometimes. Or dead fish or something.

PRILL No. I can't explain. It was worse than anything like that. Worse than anything I've ever smelled before. Much, much worse. Even Alison could smell it: she went all red and rigid and wouldn't stop screaming. I almost couldn't breathe. I know it sounds silly but I thought I was going to die. It was like when they clamp that mask over your face when they give you gas.

COLIN You didn't say anything yesterday.

The sounds of digging cease.

PRILL No. I was really scared, but I felt silly. I couldn't tell Mum and Dad I was frightened of a smell, could I.

Oliver *enters from outside to get himself a glass of water.*

PRILL Hi, Olly. You look hot.

COLIN Why don't you take that jumper off?

OLIVER   I'm all right, thank you. I'm not too hot.

PRILL   What have you been doing?

OLIVER   I'm making a den.

COLIN   What sort of den?

OLIVER   Well, I'm digging a pit in the ground, and then I'm going to roof it over with branches and grass. Uncle said I was allowed.

COLIN   Where is it?

OLIVER   Round the side. Where they're going to build the garage. The workmen have left spades there and everything.

COLIN   What d'you want a den for?

OLIVER   I just do.

COLIN   A bit babyish, isn't it?

PRILL   'Course it's not, Colin. Leave him alone. Anyway he's younger than you.

OLIVER   It'll be very good. I'm going to make it really deep. I want to be able to stand up in it.

COLIN   You'll still be digging when we're packing up to leave.

PRILL   We're going down to the beach for a swim, Oll. Do you want to come?

OLIVER   I can't swim.

COLIN   Can't swim — at your age!

PRILL   Well, you could paddle, couldn't you? It'll cool you down a bit.

OLIVER   Are you sure you want me to come?

PRILL   Of course we do.   *Giving a sharp look at* **Colin.**

OLIVER   All right then.

COLIN   And we've got to look around for Jessie on the way. She's done a Houdini.

SCENE FOUR

Donal's garden and caravan. Day. **Colin, Prill** *and* **Oliver** *approach the garden — a large plot given over entirely to potatoes.*

COLIN   *calling*   Jessie! Jessie! Come on, girl!

PRILL *pointing to the caravan* Ooh, look. Someone must live there.

OLIVER Whoever it is has got a big potato patch.

COLIN How d'you know they're potatoes?

OLIVER I can recognise them by the leaves.

PRILL Don't you know what potato plants look like, Colin?

COLIN How should I? When we buy potatoes out of the shop they don't have leaves on, do they?

OLIVER *stooping down to examine a plant* Hey! Look at this!

COLIN What is it?

OLIVER It's some sort of beetle. I've never seen one like this before.

COLIN Let's see.

PRILL It's all stripey — it's beautiful.

OLIVER There's lots, look.

Oliver *takes a matchbox out of his pocket and puts two of the beetles into it.*

PRILL What are you doing?

OLIVER I want to look them up in my book to see what sort they are.

COLIN Well do that later. I want to get down to the sea before I melt.

OLIVER *examining further along the row* Look, they're eating all the potato leaves. I think we ought to tell whoever lives here about this.

COLIN It's nothing to do with us. Come on!

PRILL He probably knows, Olly. He lives here. He must know more about gardening than you.

OLIVER Well I think we have a civic duty to tell the owner.

COLIN *scornfully* Civic duty! What are you on about?

Oliver *goes to the caravan door and knocks.* **Colin** *and* **Prill** *watch him with astonishment.* **Oliver** *waits then knocks again. The door opens and* **Donal** *appears, looking as though he's just woken.*

DONAL What d'you want, coming here! Who are you, at all! Go on! Go on! Get away, will yous! There's been enough of it,

I'm telling yous! Leave a soul in peace, can't yous, coming round here! God help me!

OLIVER *retreating* I just thought you ought to know...

DONAL Away! Away! Before I take a stick to yous! Away!

Colin, Prill *and* **Oliver** *withdraw hurriedly.* **Donal** *goes back inside and slams the door.*

COLIN See! That was your fault!

OLIVER I couldn't help it if he wouldn't listen.

COLIN Let's go down for this swim now before you get us into any more trouble.

OLIVER I'm not coming.

PRILL Oh, come on, Olly.

OLIVER I'm going back to the house.

COLIN Good riddance.

PRILL All right then. See you later.

OLIVER See you.

COLIN Come on, Prill, for goodness sake.

SCENE FIVE

Prill's bedroom. Night. **Colin** *enters.* **Prill** *is in bed. Both are agitated. The room is lit by moonlight which floods through the window. In the background we hear the* **Baby** *crying throughout.*

COLIN Are you awake, Prill?

PRILL Yes.

COLIN Can I come and talk to you a minute?

PRILL Yes. All right.

Prill *sits up.* **Colin** *sits on the side of her bed.*

COLIN It's so hot I couldn't sleep. My bed was soaked with sweat but I had to close the window because of the smell.

PRILL So you smelt it too.

COLIN The stench is terrible. What can it be?

PRILL I don't know. It's gone again now. But I'm frightened to open my window in case it comes back.

COLIN I felt really ill.

9

PRILL Me too.

COLIN And there's something else funny. My bedclothes felt really horrible so I put the light on, and they're all covered in a greeny-blue mouldy fuzz.

PRILL Eugh!

COLIN Are yours all right?

PRILL Put the light on.

Colin *puts on the light and they examine Prill's sheets which they find have no mould on them.*

PRILL They seem to be all right.

COLIN So were Olly's.

PRILL Is he awake?

COLIN No. He's fast asleep. He doesn't even look hot. And do you know what he's done? — he's pinched some of that loony old man's potato plants. He's got them in a glass jar beside his bed with all those stripey insects crawling all over them.

PRILL Eugh! How revolting. I'd be scared they'd get out and crawl all over me.

COLIN Well how do you think I feel trying to sleep next to that?

PRILL Poor Colin.

COLIN And I can't go back and get into those mouldy sheets, Prill. Can I lie down on your rug?

PRILL Oh, yes please. I wish you would. My blankets are on the floor, there, look, at the end of the bed.

COLIN It's much too hot for a blanket.

PRILL Not to **cover** you. I mean, fold them up to lie on so it'll be a bit softer.

COLIN That's a good idea.

Colin *makes himself a bed out of the blankets, puts the light out, and lies down.*

PRILL I'm glad you're here. I was frightened to go back to sleep.

COLIN Why?

PRILL I had this terrible nightmare.

COLIN What about?

PRILL Well, I was looking out of the window, and where the drive is, there was just a field. It was pouring with rain and there was someone crawling about out there in the mud. And whatever was supposed to be growing out there was all black and rotten and stinking of that smell. And this person who was crawling about on her hands and knees, was an old-looking woman in rags, really skinny, like a stick insect, and she was getting handfuls of wet mud and stuffing them into her mouth and trying to eat them. It was really awful.

Pause.

COLIN   Do you think it's us?

PRILL   What d'you mean?

COLIN   I don't know. Perhaps we're ill. Perhaps we've got some disease that's affecting our imaginations.

PRILL   Well if we have, it sounds as if Alison's got it as well. Listen to her. She's been going on like that all night.

COLIN   Yeah, but that wally, Oliver, seems to be all right.

PRILL   We could see if we've got a temperature. There's a thermometer in the first aid kit in the kitchen.

COLIN   O.K.

Colin *and* **Prill** *get up and exit.*

SCENE SIX

Kitchen. Night. **Colin** *and* **Prill** *enter and search through drawers until they find the first aid kit. The* **Baby's** *cries can be heard throughout.* **Prill** *puts the thermometer into* **Colin's** *mouth.*

PRILL   Mum can't be getting much sleep.

COLIN   *with the thermometer in*   Especially with Dad not here to help.

PRILL   Shall we make her a cup of tea?

COLIN   Good idea.

Prill *fills the electric kettle and switches it on, then fetches the milk jug from the fridge.*

PRILL   Eugh! We can't use this!

COLIN   What's the matter?

PRILL   It's off.

11

COLIN It can't be. I got it from the farm straight after milking. It was all right at supper time.

PRILL Well it's off now. Look.

Colin *takes the thermometer out of his mouth and lays it on the table. He takes the jug to the sink and peers into it. The surface is blue with mould. He tips the milk into the sink. The contents have solidified and the shiny gell slides out.*

PRILL It's nearly solid. And smell it!

COLIN It's making me feel sick again.

Colin *hastily dumps the jug in the sink and he and* **Prill** *retreat across the room.*

COLIN There must be something wrong with the fridge.

PRILL No. The motor's working all right.

Prill *goes to the fridge and feels inside.*

PRILL It's cold. There's ice and everything.

COLIN I wish Dad was here.

PRILL Have you got a temperature?

Colin *picks up the thermometer and looks at it.*

COLIN No.

PRILL It's this house. I wish we'd never come.

Day Three
SCENE SEVEN

Kitchen. Day. **Colin** *and* **Prill** *are eating breakfast. In the background we hear sounds of digging.* **Mum** *stands in the kitchen doorway.*

MUM Alison's just dropped off at last. I'm going back to bed for a while. Are you all right?

COLIN Yes.

PRILL Yes thanks, Mum.

Mum *exits.*

PRILL Don't say anything to Mum about the mouldy sheets and everything. She's all worried and worn out already.

COLIN Anyway, they're all right now.

12

PRILL   How d'you mean, **all right**?

COLIN   The sheets have dried and all the mould's disappeared.

PRILL   Perhaps you just dreamt it.

COLIN   *uncertainly*   Perhaps.

PRILL   I'm going to phone Dad, anyway.

COLIN   You're not supposed to phone him at work.

PRILL   I know. But he said he was going to phone every morning, and he hasn't.

Prill *dials the number.*

COLIN   That's 'cos he's probably too busy. He'll phone when he gets a minute.

PRILL   Oh, no!

Prill *tries dialling again.*

COLIN   What's the matter?

PRILL   Nothing!

Prill *presses the cradle up and down frantically. Outside, the digging ceases.*

PRILL   *listening into the phone.*   No dialling tone. It's dead as a dodo. No wonder Dad can't get through.

COLIN   That's all we need.

Oliver *enters carrying a tray of his 'finds' which he places on the kitchen table.*

PRILL   What have you got there, Olly?

OLIVER   Pieces of china, mostly.

COLIN   What's that — money?

OLIVER   Just an old ha'penny.

COLIN   How old?

OLIVER   I don't know till I've cleaned it up.

PRILL   And what are these white bits?

OLIVER   Pieces of clay pipe, I should think.

COLIN   Why don't you take your jumper off? How are you going to get brown with a vest and shirt and jumper and long trousers and everything? People won't even know you've been on holiday.

OLIVER   I'm all right, thank you.

PRILL   Are you going to wash the dirt off these?

OLIVER   No! You mustn't wash things like this. They might disintegrate. I've brought an old toothbrush. You have to brush the dirt away very, very gently.

COLIN   You're a right little know-all, you are.

PRILL   Leave him alone, Colin. Remember what Dad said: make allowances.

Oliver *gives* **Prill** *an angry look.*

SCENE EIGHT

The O'Malley kitchen. Day. **Mrs O'Malley** *is washing up.*
Kevin *is cleaning and trying to repair his motorbike carburretor on a newspaper on the table. There is a knock at the door.*

MRS O'MALLEY   Come in.

Colin *enters.*

COLIN   Hello, Mrs O'Malley.

Colin *exchanges nods with* **Kevin.**

MRS O'MALLEY   Hello. Colin, isn't it?

COLIN   My mum sent me to say our phone isn't working.

MRS O'MALLEY   Is that so? Kevin, try ours.

Kevin *gets up, wiping his hands on a rag, and crosses the room to pick up their phone.*

KEVIN   Sure, it sounds all right.

MRS O'MALLEY   Tell your mother I'll phone the exchange, so I will, and ask them to send someone. Usually all the phones go off together when we have a bad storm.

COLIN   Do you often have storms?

MRS O'MALLEY   Being on the west coast here, we get our share, don't we Kevin.

KEVIN   Aye, but we haven't had a bad one since March.

MRS O'MALLEY   Oh, that was a fierce wind, to be sure. I'm surprised old Donal's caravan wasn't blown clean away. And how's your little one today?

14

COLIN   She's not very well. She's been crying all night.

MRS O'MALLEY   Oh Jesus Mary. Your poor mother. She must be worn out.

COLIN   It's probably just this awful heat.

MRS O'MALLEY   The heat, is it? But it's not been so specially hot, has it? I haven't noticed.

COLIN   And Mum said if you have any to spare, could we buy some more milk?

MRS O'MALLEY   More milk? You're surely great milk drinkers down there.

COLIN   Our milk was off last night.

MRS O'MALLEY   *Shocked*   Off, was it? How could that be? I'm so sorry, tell your mother. It must have been Donal. We let him help in the dairy in the evenings, so he still feels he's of use, but he sometimes gets a little confused these days. You probably got some old milk by mistake. I'll slip across to the dairy and get you some more.

Mrs O'Malley *exits.*

COLIN   Is Donal that old man in the caravan?

KEVIN   Aye.

COLIN   He's a bit fierce, isn't he?

KEVIN   You mustn't mind him. He doesn't like changes and new faces.

COLIN   Has he always lived around here?

KEVIN   He came from Donegal when he was a young man, and he's worked all his life as a labourer on our farm — first with my grandad and then with my dad. He was a great one for the crack when he was younger. He was always full of stories about his grandmother, Bridget, who'd been left a widow on a tiny farm up in Donegal with eleven small children to raise. He's a bit odd now, like. A bit crotchety.

Colin *is not very interested. There is a short, awkward silence.*

COLIN   Are there any good places to explore round here?

KEVIN   There's the yellow tunnel. I used to go there a lot.

COLIN   What's that?

KEVIN   When it's low tide, you can go along the shore. Otherwise you have to go over the top. But at low tide you can walk right along as far as Ballimagliesh Strand, then

15

you climb up to the ruined chapel that sits right on the cliff edge. Lots of people go there for picnics.

COLIN   But what about the tunnel?

KEVIN   Well, instead of using the cliff path, you climb up from the beach through a crack in the rocks. You come out in the old graveyard by the chapel walls.

COLIN   Do you need ropes?

KEVIN   No. There's plenty of footholds. But it's dark as hell. It's like being in an old chimney. Did you ever read that book about the chimney sweeps' boys in London?

COLIN   No. I don't read much.

KEVIN   I read a lot. I suppose it's because we're a bit isolated here.

Mrs O'Malley *enters with milk in a can.*

MRS O'MALLEY   Here you are, dear. Give this to your mother, and tell her I'm very sorry. And I'll see about the telephone this minute.

SCENE NINE

Oliver's hole. Day. **Oliver** *stops digging as* **Prill** *arrives. He is surly and unfriendly.*

PRILL   Why don't you come, Olly?

OLIVER   No thanks. I'm busy.

PRILL   But it'll be a lovely picnic. Kevin's told Colin about this great place. And there's a ruined chapel and everything.

OLIVER   I know. He told me. I do want to see it, but at another time. I'd rather stay here at the moment — I've started making some really good finds.

PRILL   Let's see them.

OLIVER   You haven't got time now. I'll show you later. And anyway, I want to go and see old Donal again.

PRILL   You must be crackers. What on earth do you want to see him for?

OLIVER   I have to warn him about that pest on his potatoes.

PRILL   I'm sure he knows more about potato pests than you do — he's been a farm worker all his life.

OLIVER   I expect he does. But he probably hasn't noticed. Perhaps his eyesight isn't as good as it used to be. He **is** nearly ninety.

PRILL   You shouldn't meddle in other people's affairs.

OLIVER   Sometimes you have to meddle. If someone had meddled in Germany, Hitler might not have come to power — that's what my dad says.

PRILL   I don't know what you're talking about.

OLIVER   If there's a drastic problem, you sometimes have to find drastic solutions.

PRILL   *pulling a face at him*   Well make sure you don't do anything drastic while we're out.

OLIVER   All right. Anyway, I have to get on now.

PRILL   You're sure you'll be all right on your own?

OLIVER   *beginning to dig.*   Yes. Of course I will.

PRILL   Mum's left you some cake and an apple on the table. See you.

SCENE TEN

The O'Malley's kitchen. Day. **Mrs O'Malley** *is preparing the evening meal.* **Oliver** *sits dejectedly at the table, an untouched glass of lemonade and slice of cake in front of him. He has been crying.* **Kevin** *enters followed by Prill's and Colin's* **Mum.**

KEVIN   Here she is, Mam. They're just back.

Kevin *exits.*

MUM   Hello, Mrs O'Malley. Whatever's wrong?

MRS O'MALLEY   Nothing serious, Mrs Blakeman. Sit down, sit down. I'm just after making a cup of tea.

Mum *sits opposite* **Oliver. Mrs O'Malley** *sets about making a pot of tea.*

MUM   Oliver, what have you been up to?

MRS O'MALLEY   Sure, the young lad was only trying to help. He thought there was a pest on Donal's potatoes and he burned the field.

MUM   *horrified*   Oliver!

OLIVER   There **was** a pest. You can ask Colin and Prill. I showed them. The crop was infested with potato beetle.

MRS O'MALLEY If it **was** the beetle, that would be a serious thing. Mr O'Malley will report it just in case. But it's very rare nowadays.

MUM Oliver! It was probably ladybirds or something.

OLIVER *scornfully* I know what a ladybird looks like! It **was** potato beetle. I checked it with my book.

MUM But even so, you shouldn't just burn other people's crops. Why didn't you just **tell** somebody?

OLIVER I tried. I tried to tell Donal, but he wouldn't listen. Colin and Prill were there. And I went again to tell him, even though he'd threatened me, but there was nobody there. I didn't know how long he was going to be away. And if action wasn't taken at once it would have spread to Mr O'Malley's fields.

MUM But that doesn't mean you should have acted on your own.

OLIVER But you don't realise how important it is. There was a famine here once when the potato crop was lost. A million people died.

MRS O'MALLEY That's true enough, Oliver. Famine's a terrible thing. But that was the blight, not potato beetle. And that was a long time ago.

OLIVER But there are still famines. There's people dying of hunger every day. And famine could be avoided if people acted — that's what my dad says.

MUM I'm sure that's right, Oliver. But I don't think he meant you to act without consulting other people.

MRS O'MALLEY And there was another little complication. Being so dry, and with the breeze coming off the sea, the fire got a wee bit out of control, so it did.

MUM Oh? What happened?

MRS O'MALLEY The kindling stacked against Donal's caravan caught fire and the caravan was slightly damaged.

MUM Oliver!

OLIVER I'm sorry. I couldn't help it.

MRS O'MALLEY It's not serious. My husband saw the smoke, thanks be to God, and he and Kevin put the fire out.

OLIVER And me. I helped.

MRS O'MALLEY   And Oliver too. There isn't a lot of damage done. Donal's gone to stay at Father Hagan's while Mr O'Malley does a few repairs. It'll only take him a few hours. The caravan will be as good as new by tomorrow evening.

OLIVER   I said I'll pay. I'll write to my mum and ask her to send the money — then I'll pay it back out of my pocket money. I don't care how long it takes.

MUM   No, Oliver! Don't you dare mention it to your mother. I know my sister. She'd be out here on the next boat and you'd be carted off back home. We'll sort out the finances. I'll speak to your uncle as soon as the phone is back on.

MRS O'MALLEY   Oh, the phone is on. The man came this afternoon.

MUM   Thank goodness for that, anyway. I'll phone my husband. And I'll get a doctor to come and have a look at Alison. She's not well, and she seems to be losing weight.

MRS O'MALLEY   Don't trouble yourself about the doctor. I'll phone for you. Now here's a nice cup of tea. Dr O'Keefe is on holiday at the moment, but old Dr Donovan looks after things while he's away. He's a bit of a grump, but I'll get him to come out tomorrow. Now then, dinner's nearly ready. Would you all like to come for a bite with us?

MUM   Oh, no, thank you, Mrs O'Malley. I'm sure we've been enough trouble already. As soon as I've drunk my tea we'll get back. Poor Prill's trying to comfort the baby. And I want to telephone my husband. Perhaps he could phone Mr O'Malley and talk about the cost of the fire damage.

MRS O'MALLEY   Oh, don't bother about that, Mrs Blakeman. Sure, it's nothing at all.

SCENE ELEVEN

Kitchen. Day. **Colin** *and* **Prill** *are laying the table.* **Mum** *and* **Oliver** *enter.*

PRILL   Hello, Mum. Alison's gone to sleep at last.

MUM   How did you manage that? You are a clever girl.

COLIN   What was all that about, Mum? Why have you been so long?

MUM   Nothing, dear. The good news is, the phone's on again.

PRILL   Great.   *Urgently*   Can we phone Dad? Can I phone **now**?

MUM   Yes, dear. I want to speak to him before I do anything else.

Prill *picks up the receiver, dials the number, listens, jiggles the cradle buttons up and down.*

OLIVER   I'm going to bed, Aunty Jeannie.

MUM   Aren't you going to have some supper first, love?

OLIVER   No thank you. I just want to go to bed.

MUM   All right, love. Sleep well.

OLIVER   I'm sorry about what happened, Aunty.

MUM   Don't worry, dear. All's well that ends well.

Oliver *exits.*

COLIN   What did happen?

PRILL   This phone's still dead.

The **Baby** *begins to cry in the other room, and continues throughout the scene.*

MUM   But the engineer's been.

PRILL   *beginning to cry*   I don't think if they sent a thousand engineers it would make any difference. It's not the phone that's wrong. It's this house. There's something wrong with this house.

Mum *picks up the phone to listen for herself.*

MUM   Now don't be silly, dear. Telephones are always going wrong — especially in the country.

PRILL   Why don't we go up to the O'Malley's and use theirs?

MUM   I don't think so, dear. They must have had enough of us for one day — especially after Oliver's little escapade.

COLIN   What **was** Oliver's little escapade? Why are you being so secretive?

MUM   I'm not. I'll tell you in a minute. Oh, listen to that baby. She'll just have to cry for a while. I can't cope.

PRILL   I'll feed Jessie.

Prill *exits.*

COLIN   What are we going to have for supper, Mum? I'm starving.

MUM   I don't know. I should have thought, after all the food you put away on the picnic, you wouldn't feel hungry again for a week.

COLIN   I've got real hunger pains in my stomach.

MUM   There's plenty of potatoes. What about chips and something? We'll try out their new chip pan.

COLIN   Great. I'll peel the spuds.

MUM   Thank you, Colin. That'll be a great help.

COLIN   Where are they?

MUM   In the utility room. In the carrier bag on the tiled counter.

Colin *exits.*

MUM   *to herself*   Well, they've certainly got all mod cons. Electric tin opener — I wonder how you use this?

Colin *re-enters with the carrier bag which he puts on the table. He looks shocked and ill.*

MUM   What on earth's the matter? You've gone as white as a sheet.

COLIN   Are these the ones?

Prill *re-enters.* **Mum** *goes to look at the potatoes.*

PRILL   There's something wrong with Jessie, Mum. She hadn't touched her breakfast and it had gone all mouldy. And she won't eat her supper either. I've never known her not eat before. She's usually a real pig. She's just lying there. She wouldn't even get up when I called her.   **Prill** *realises there's something wrong*   What's the matter? What's that **smell**?

COLIN   The potatoes.

PRILL   What about them?

MUM   They were all right last night. We had them for supper.

PRILL   It was the night before. It was when Dad was here.

MUM   Well they were all right **then**.

COLIN   *horrified*   They're just black slime.   *Nearly crying*   The bag's full of black slime — it's oozing out, look.

PRILL   It smells like rotten eggs.

MUM   All right, now. Don't get upset. Just close up the bag,

21

Colin, and throw it out. And move the rubbish bin well away from the house.

Colin *takes the bag at arm's length and goes to the door.*

MUM   What am I going to give you to fill you up now, I wonder?

PRILL   I don't want anything, Mum. That stink — I couldn't eat a thing.

COLIN   Nor me.

Colin *exits.* **Mum** *stands looking helpless and bewildered.*

SCENE TWELVE

Colin's bedroom. Night. We hear the sounds of a thunderstorm outside and the **Baby's** *crying from another room.* **Colin** *is standing by the open window, staring out.* **Prill** *comes crashing in, distraught.*

PRILL   *seeing* **Colin**   What's the matter? What are you doing?

COLIN   What's the matter with **you**?

PRILL   I had a nightmare again. That old beggar woman. She was running across that field in front of the house that I dreamt about before. It looked like that potato field after Oliver burned it, and it stank like those rotten potatoes, only worse. She fell on her face in the mud. Then she got up and came right up to my window. She looked like a skeleton — and . . . and her face was just like the face of that nasty old man in the caravan.

While talking, **Prill** *has taken hold of* **Colin's** *hand.*

PRILL   You're shaking all over. What's the matter?

COLIN   It wasn't a dream. That woman **was** peering in the window.

PRILL   What woman?

COLIN   The one you saw. The beggar woman who looks like Donal Morrissey — at first I thought it was him.

PRILL   But it couldn't have been, could it? He's staying the night up at the priest's house.

COLIN   I know.

22

PRILL I'm going to go into the village first thing in the morning and phone Dad. I want him to come back.

COLIN I think everything would be better if he did. Mum can't cope with Alison. She's going to pieces. I've never known her like this before.

PRILL We should pack up and go home. It's this place. I'm going to tell Dad.

COLIN He won't understand. He'll say it's the weather, and we're exaggerating, and we've all got a bug or something.

PRILL But we've got to **persuade** him. There's something wrong with this house. It's all modern and everything, but there's something terribly wrong here.

COLIN What do you think's happening to us?

PRILL I don't know, Col. But I'm **frightened.**

They stare at each other, open-mouthed.

Day Four
SCENE THIRTEEN

Oliver's hole. Day. **Oliver** *is digging.* **Colin** *and* **Prill** *are helping him.*

PRILL You've done a lot, Olly. You've been working hard. Ouch!

COLIN What's the matter?

PRILL I can't get this rock up. I've scraped my fingers.

COLIN I'll help.

OLIVER Kevin O'Malley said he'd bring me a sheet of corrugated iron for the roof. I don't suppose he will now though.

PRILL Have you found anything else interesting?

OLIVER Only the remains of a dog.

PRILL A **dog**?

OLIVER I think that's what it is. Just some old bones. I put them in that bin bag under the hedge.

PRILL Ugh! Do they smell?

OLIVER Not really. Do you want to see them?

PRILL **No thanks.**

COLIN How deep are you going to go, Oll?

OLIVER Well, I'd like to be able to stand up in it when the roof's on.

COLIN Stand up in it? — you must be mad!

PRILL Well, as soon as it's time for the shops to open I'm going up to the village to get some food and to phone Dad.

COLIN And as soon as it gets a bit hotter I'm going for a swim.

PRILL I thought that storm would have made it cooler, but it's muggier than ever. Ooh, look!

COLIN What?

PRILL I've found something interesting.

COLIN What is it?

PRILL I don't know.

OLIVER Let's see.

Oliver *begins to brush the dirt away carefully with his toothbrush.*

OLIVER It's pottery, I think.

PRILL I'm glad it's not another bone *Pause — she looks at Colin before she goes on* We think there's something wrong with this house, Olly.

OLIVER *still brushing — very matter of fact* Yes. I think so too. Perhaps it's haunted.

COLIN But it's a brand new house. It's not even finished yet.

OLIVER I don't think that matters. It's only in kids' stories that haunted houses are old and creaking. My father knew some people who had a poltergeist, and they lived in a brand new house — a council house.

PRILL But how can you be haunted by bad smells and . . . and by food going mouldy?

OLIVER I don't know. The reasons why places are haunted are very complicated. But I can tell you one thing: Mr Catchpole's aunt in Dorset was haunted by an old woman, and before she saw her there was always a smell of frying bacon.

COLIN Who's Mr Catchpole for heaven's sake?

OLIVER An old man who lodges in our house — he's a friend of mine.

PRILL I wouldn't mind the smell of frying bacon.

COLIN Shut up. You're making my mouth water. I'm starving.

PRILL I think it's that awful stench that keeps coming that's making us feel sick all the time.

COLIN **And** Jessie.

PRILL **And** what's making Alison ill.

COLIN **And** what keeps giving me terrible stomach cramps.

OLIVER Perhaps.

COLIN Have you smelt it, then?

OLIVER Yes.

COLIN You didn't say anything.

OLIVER You never asked me. You hardly talk to me at all.

Pause. **Colin** *and* **Prill** *exchange embarrassed looks.*

PRILL Do you think it could be the smell that's causing our nightmares?

OLIVER What sort of nightmares?

PRILL We've both been having terrible dreams, and last night we both had the same one — about this ragged old woman who looks like Donal Morrissey.

OLIVER I dreamt about him too.

PRILL *Shocked* Did you?

OLIVER Yes.

COLIN Really?

OLIVER Yes. But my father says you often dream about what you were thinking about just before you go to sleep — I don't suppose it means anything.

PRILL But why is all this happening to **us**?

OLIVER I don't know.

COLIN Perhaps we're just imagining it all.

OLIVER Oh no, I don't think so. It's like what my father is always saying.

COLIN And what's that?

OLIVER 'There are more things in heaven and earth, Horatio, than are dreamt of in your philosophy.'

COLIN And what's that supposed to mean when it's at home?

OLIVER Well, it's a saying. I think it's from Shakespeare.

COLIN   But what does it **mean**?

OLIVER   I don't know really. Just that everything is possible, I suppose, and that you shouldn't laugh at things just because you don't understand them.

COLIN   Nobody's laughing, Olly, you little twit.

PRILL   Don't be so rotten to him, Colin.

KEVIN   *calling — off stage*   Hello there. How's it going?

Colin, Prill and **Oliver** *look in* **Kevin's** *direction.*

COLIN   Hi, Kev.
PRILL   Hello.   } *Together.*
OLIVER   Hello, Kevin.

Kevin *enters, carrying a can of milk.*

KEVIN   You're up early.

COLIN   We couldn't sleep.

Kevin *puts the can down.*

KEVIN   Sure, it's the storm — all hot and humid. And the telephone lines must be down because our phone's off now. But tell your mother we phoned Dr Donovan last night and he said he'll be down today to see the wee babby — but probably not till the afternoon. How is she anyway?

PRILL   Terrible. She's been screaming all night again.

KEVIN   Well tell your mother not to worry. The doctor will be here later for sure. And if you're planning to go out, I wouldn't go too far: the forecast is for more storms.

COLIN   Great. Just great.

PRILL   I'm going to wash my hands and go up to the village. Will the shops be open yet, Kevin?

KEVIN   They will be by the time you get there.

SCENE FOURTEEN

Father Hagan's sitting room. Day. **Prill** *is lying on the settee.* **Father Hagan** *is pressing a damp cloth to her forehead.* **Prill** *is recovering from a faint. Throughout the scene she remains numbed, lifeless, and in a state of shock.*

FATHER HAGAN   Ah. How are you feeling now?

Prill *tries to sit up.*

FATHER HAGAN Stay there. Rest a little more.

PRILL Is this your house?

FATHER HAGAN It is. You fainted in the shop next door. And you were sick too. I was there at the time. You'll be all right now.

PRILL Thank you.

FATHER HAGAN We sent for Dr Donovan, but he's out on his rounds. Still, he'll be calling on your mother this afternoon to see the baby, so he can have a look at you at the same time. I'll take you home in a little while in the car.

PRILL Thank you.

FATHER HAGAN Is the baby not well?

PRILL No. She's really ill. *She starts to cry* I wanted to phone my dad but the telephone wasn't working.

FATHER HAGAN They'll soon have the phones fixed — don't worry about that. Tell me what happened in the shop.

PRILL But you were there. You must have seen.

FATHER HAGAN Yes, but. . . you tell me in your words.

PRILL Well, it all began when I was walking up here. There were two beggar children on the road.

FATHER HAGAN Beggars, you say? We've seen no beggars round here for many a year.

PRILL Well, there was a boy and a girl, about the same ages as Colin and me, all dressed in rags, and as thin as scarecrows.

FATHER HAGAN They must have been tinker children, surely, but I hadn't heard there were tinkers in the neighbourhood.

PRILL They had bare feet and their faces were all skin and bone, and small and. . . sort of hairy — like monkeys. And their eyes looked huge and staring.

FATHER HAGAN You're sure? Can this be true?

PRILL Yes. I was really frightened. And their hands were withered and bony — like claws. And they opened and closed their mouths but no words came out — just sort of low, animal noises. The boy grabbed hold of my arm and scratched me — look.

Prill *holds out her arm for* **Father Hagan** *to see.*

FATHER HAGAN   But there's no scratch marks here, my dear.

PRILL   *beginning to shout*   Well I **did** see them. It's **true**. And I saw the **baby**.

FATHER HAGAN   There, there. Don't get upset. I'm sure you did. And what baby was this?

PRILL   The one in the shop.

FATHER HAGAN   In the shop?

PRILL   Didn't you see it?

FATHER HAGAN   Tell me what happened in the shop.

PRILL   I was waiting by the counter. I saw you by the door talking to a woman.

FATHER HAGAN   That's right. So I was.

PRILL   Then this ragged woman pushed past me and was begging for a loaf of bread. The shop man asked her how much she had and when she told him he said that wasn't enough. She began to cry and plead with him. She said, 'For the love of God, spare me something. Take all I've got.' And she held her hand out clenched tight.

FATHER HAGAN   And then?

PRILL   The shop man prised open her fingers and there was nothing in her hand. He said, 'I'm sorry. You've no money at all, and God knows we've got little enough ourselves.' Then the shop door slammed and buckets and things started falling about.

FATHER HAGAN   That's true enough — it was the wind springing up and causing havoc.

PRILL   And she shrieked and grabbed a loaf of bread off the counter, and she screamed out, 'Take what I have, and may God help me!' She dumped this bundle of rags on the counter and turned and ran past me with the bread, and I recognised her.

FATHER HAGAN   Who was it?

PRILL   It's this woman I see at night stumbling about in the field outside my bedroom.

FATHER HAGAN   But Priscilla, dear, there's a gravel driveway outside your bedroom.

PRILL   I know. But not always. Sometimes it's a field. Earth and mud and a few blackened stalks and this terrible stench.

FATHER HAGAN   But you mentioned a baby.

PRILL   Yes. . . The bundle of rags on the counter. I unwrapped it, and. . .   *She is crying more and more*   and. . . and it was a dead baby. It looked like Alison, except it was just skin over bones, and it stank awful, like rotten meat.

FATHER HAGAN   There, there, child. Be calm now. Don't distress yourself. It's all over now. You were hallucinating. I was there. I saw it. A delivery man brought in a ham while you were waiting. It was wrapped in a muslin cloth. I saw him carry it in with my own eyes.

PRILL   *becoming hysterical*   But I **wasn't** imagining it! I **did** see it! I **did**!

FATHER HAGAN   You weren't imagining it, no. You did see it. What you were seeing was real enough. But it was an hallucination, nevertheless. Be calm now. I'll take you home in a minute so you're sure to be there before the doctor comes. And we'll talk about this again — when you're less fraught.

PRILL   *stopping crying*   I'm sorry. I feel a bit better now.

FATHER HAGAN   Have you been to Ireland before?

PRILL   No. This is the first time.

FATHER HAGAN   Do you know any of the history of Ireland?

PRILL   No. At school we don't do Ireland. Anyway we're only up to the Normans. Oliver knows some history though. He's got a book about it.

FATHER HAGAN   Has he told you any stories from it? Any incidents that happened in the past?

PRILL   No.

FATHER HAGAN   Or have you read any novels? Or seen anything on television?

PRILL   No. I don't think so.

FATHER HAGAN   Has Oliver any Irish connections, do you know?

PRILL   I don't know. He's adopted. No one knows who his real parents were.

FATHER HAGAN   He's an unusual little boy, so he is, digging his hole, and burning the potato field. A real individual.

PRILL   Yes. I suppose he is.

FATHER HAGAN   Well, Priscilla, do you feel ready to go home now?

PRILL   Yes please. I feel much better now, thank you.

SCENE FIFTEEN

Kitchen. Day. **Prill, Colin** *and* **Oliver** *are drinking tea. The* **Baby** *can be heard screaming in the next room.*

COLIN   No wonder she's screaming. I didn't like the look of that doctor.

OLIVER   He's just tired and old.

PRILL   Too old. He gave me the creeps. I've not having him look at me.

COLIN   And he needn't have been so rude — barging in like that without being asked. I think he was half-drunk.

OLIVER   He's obviously busy. He just wants to get his rounds finished.

Dr Donovan *and* **Mum** *enter. The* **Baby** *is still yelling in the next room.*

DR DONOVAN   *irritably*   The temperature is normal. So is the pulse. She's not refusing food, you say, and the bowels are in order. She's a bit thin — but that's all to the good: fat babies are unhealthy.   *He dumps two bottles on the table*   The pink — give her a couple of spoonfuls at bedtime if she's playing up. The white — that's for tummy upsets — you never know, may just be hatching a little bug. Come up to the surgery in a couple of days if you're still not happy about her. She'll be as fit as a fiddle in a few days, no doubt. Now, wasn't there another invalid?

PRILL   No, Mum. I'm all right now.

MUM   Are you sure, dear?

PRILL   Yes. I'm sure. *She backs away from the doctor.*

DR DONOVAN   She looks fine to me, and if she feels all right, well — that's it then. I'll wish you a good day.

MUM   Thank you, Doctor.

DR DONOVAN   I'll see myself out.   *He exits.*

MUM   *After a pause*   That's that then.

PRILL   He wasn't much help, was he.

COLIN   He definitely looked drunk to me.

PRILL   I know what this is.   *She unscrews the top of the pink bottle and sniffs*   It's baby asprin in a kind of syrup. This won't do any good.

MUM   I know. It's just happy juice. You both had it as babies. It doesn't cure anything.

COLIN   You forgot to ask the doctor about Jessie, Mum.

MUM   I didn't forget, dear, but how could I ask a man like that? You saw him. Perhaps Mrs O'Malley's got something — but I don't like to keep pestering her. I'll speak to your father tomorrow. Somebody's got to have a phone that works. Surely the whole of Ireland can't be cut off! Anyway, I think I'll have a bath. Can you cope with Alison between you for a while? I'm just about at the end of my tether. I don't think I can stand much more of her today.   *She exits.*

Colin and **Prill** *stare at each other dismayed, frightened. After a while* **Oliver** *gets up.*

OLIVER   *very upset*   I hate it when Alison cries. I'll go.

Oliver *exits.* **Prill** *and* **Colin** *exchange surprised looks.*

COLIN   At least we've got some medicines now. They may help Alison sleep so Mum can get some rest.

The **Baby's** *cries subside.*

PRILL   You heard what Mum said. They won't do any good. I know they won't.

The **Baby's** *cries cease altogether.*

PRILL   I don't think it's an ordinary illness that you can cure with medicines anyway.

Oliver *re-enters carrying the* **Baby** *gently and cooing softly to her.*

PRILL   Gosh, Olly. How did you do that?

Oliver *shrugs and continues to coo. He walks up and down the kitchen cuddling the* **Baby.**

COLIN   Huh. She won't shut up for me.

OLIVER   I think your mother should take her to the hospital.

PRILL Why, Oll? What could **they** do? You heard the doctor — she's not got a temperature or anything.

COLIN You were sticking up for the stupid old doctor just now. If she needed to go to the hospital he would have said so.

OLIVER He's an old man, that's all. I don't think he recognised what was wrong.

COLIN So what do you think is wrong, then, Clever Dick?

OLIVER I think she's starving.

COLIN Oh, come on. That's ridiculous.

OLIVER There's an illness — I don't know what it's called; it's very rare — when food you eat doesn't do you any good. It's something to do with your blood and things. You just keep losing weight.

COLIN And then what?

OLIVER Then. . . you die.

COLIN How can that be? How on earth do you know that? You think you're a know-all, you do, but you don't know anything.

OLIVER My mother was a nurse. . .

COLIN Yes, we know that.

OLIVER When she worked on the intensive care unit at St Thomas's. . .

COLIN Oh, shut up, will you. We've heard enough from you for one day.

Oliver *gives a hopeless shrug.*

Day Five
SCENE SIXTEEN

Kitchen. Day. **Mum, Prill** *and* **Oliver** *are standing around, all somewhat agitated.*

MUM She's lost ever such a lot of weight, Prill.

PRILL How did you weigh her?

MUM It was Oliver's idea. He got me to weigh myself on the bathroom scales and then weigh myself again holding Alison.

OLIVER And I just deducted one from the other.

32

PRILL Oh, very clever. Well, have you got any brilliant ideas about what we can eat for breakfast?

MUM Colin should be back with some bread soon.

PRILL I'm so **hungry**, Mum.

MUM I know, dear.

OLIVER It was awful in the night — going to bed without anything to eat — I couldn't sleep.

PRILL Nor me.

MUM Well you can begin to understand what it must be like for people who are really starving: we only missed one meal.

PRILL It was a terrible storm, wasn't it.

MUM I suppose that's why the electricity's off.

PRILL Have you packed your things?

MUM I don't need much. I've packed a case for the baby and put my things in there. I do hope Colin won't be long.

There is a knock at the door. **Prill** *opens it.*

PRILL Come in, Mrs O'Malley.

MRS O'MALLEY Hello, children. Good morning, Mrs Blakeman. How are you all? *She enters carrying a bag and the milk.*

MUM Alison's still bad. But at least she's fallen asleep now. Sheer exhaustion, I think. I'm going to take her to hospital. Colin's gone for a taxi.

MRS O'MALLEY Yes. He called in on the way up. I was so sorry to hear about the poor little mite. Sligo General is the nearest. I told Colin to go to Danny's Bar. Young Danny will drive you, to be sure.

MUM And the electricity seems to be off.

MRS O'MALLEY Yes. You do seem to be having a time of it. It's not much of a holiday for you, to be sure. It's not always so chaotic here, believe me. The storm did a lot of damage in the night. The power is only off until the maintenance men have completed their repairs.

MUM Will they be finished today, do you know?

MRS O'MALLEY Oh, yes, God willing. It shouldn't be a long job.

MUM Because the children will be here on their own tonight.

MRS O'MALLEY Oh, dear, will they? And we're away

ourselves for two days. I brought the milk myself to tell you. There should be enough here to last — if not, you can get more from Donal. He'll be doing the milking for us with a neighbour's lad to help him.

MUM Do you think the milk will be all right?

Pause. **Mrs O'Malley** *looks at* **Mum** *in some surprise.*

MRS O'MALLEY Of course, why shouldn't it?

MUM It was just that it was off again yesterday — almost solid. I think the dog might have drunk some — perhaps that's why she's so sick today.

MRS O'MALLEY Jesus, Mary and Joseph! Off again? What can that old man be playing at! I'm very sorry, Mrs Blakeman. Indeed I am.

Mrs O'Malley *takes the lid off the milk can and smells the milk.*

MRS O'MALLEY This is this morning's, right enough. Nothing to worry about today.

PRILL But the fridge isn't working.

MRS O'MALLEY That's all right. Stand the can in a bucket of cold water in the utility room — it's cool enough in there. Just till the electric's on again. Oh, and here's some bread we won't be needing — and while I was baking yesterday I made a cake for you. I know how children love a home-made cake.

MUM Thank you, Mrs O'Malley. You're so kind. What would we have done without you?

MRS O'MALLEY Not at all, my dear. Now I must be away. They'll all be waiting in the car.

Prill *opens the door for her.*

MRS O'MALLEY Oh, and here's your Colin, now. *She exits.*

MRS O'MALLEY *off stage* Hello, Colin. Was everything all right?

COLIN *off stage* Yes, thank you, Mrs O'Malley.

Colin *enters.*

MUM Where's the taxi, Colin?

COLIN It'll be here any minute. I thought it would catch me up on the road.

MUM *peevishly*   But why is it taking so long?

COLIN   Don't worry, Mum. Young Danny was just going to have a bite of breakfast.

PRILL *looking out of the window*   There's a car coming now, Mum. It's just turned into the track.

MUM   Thank goodness. I'll fetch Alison.

OLIVER   I'll get your cases for you, Aunty Jeannie.

MUM   Thank you, Oliver. There's only the one. It's down beside the bed.

Mum *and* **Oliver** *exit.*

PRILL   You just got back in time, Colin. It's started raining again.

COLIN   We can have some breakfast as soon as they've gone. I got a loaf and some bacon.

PRILL   And Mrs O'Malley brought us a loaf as well. And a cake.

COLIN   Ah. That's lucky.

PRILL   Why?

COLIN   Well, there wouldn't have been much for three of us off my loaf.

PRILL *shocked*   Why — have you been eating it on the way?

COLIN *sheepishly*   Just a nibble or two.

PRILL   I bet you've scoffed half the loaf.

COLIN   I couldn't help it. It's lovely new bread — still warm.

PRILL   Did you manage to get a taxi easily?

COLIN   Yes. It was funny though. I went into Danny's bar, and there was this tiny old woman, as fat as a barrel, behind the bar tucking into a huge plateful of bacon and potato. My mouth was really watering. She said Young Danny was upstairs in bed but she'd call him, so I thought I'd be able to pinch some of the food off her plate.

PRILL   Colin!

COLIN   Well I was famished. But she just picked up the phone on the counter beside her plate and bellowed at him to get out of bed.

Mum *carrying the* **Baby,** *and* **Oliver** *carrying the case, re-enter. A car horn beeps from outside.* **Prill** *opens the door and* *signals to the driver.*

MUM Give me the case, Oliver. Don't come outside anybody — you'll get soaked. *She kisses each in turn* Bye bye, my loves. All look after each other. I'll be back tomorow. You're sure you'll be all right now?

PRILL *putting on a brave face* Of course we will, Mum.

Mum *exits. They close the door because the rain is coming in, and crowd round a window to watch and wave.*

PRILL Is that Young Danny?

COLIN Yes.

PRILL But he's older than our dad.

COLIN I know. But that's what everybody calls him.

OLIVER It doesn't look like a very reliable car.

COLIN It's probably only held together by rust and sellotape.

PRILL I hope it'll get there all right.

COLIN These country people with old cars are mechanical geniuses.

PRILL *suddenly distraught* Oh, no!

COLIN What's the matter?

PRILL Look!

COLIN What?

PRILL The two beggar children!

COLIN Where?

PRILL In the middle of the road! Can't he **see** them?

COLIN Where, Prill?

PRILL There! There! Oh, no! *She screams* He's run right over them! *She presses her hands over her face.*

OLIVER I can't see any children, Prill.

PRILL *opening her eyes* Oh, there they are. They're all right.

Oliver *and* **Colin** *exchange looks.* **Prill** *turns to look at them.*

PRILL I don't understand. They were standing right in front of the car.

OLIVER Who were, Prill?

PRILL Those children again.

COLIN But where are they?

PRILL *she turns back to the window* Oh. *Sounding embarrassed and bewildered* They've gone. But they **were** there — a boy and girl about our age, in rags like torn sacking.

COLIN *pause, then quietly* I saw them too.

OLIVER Where?

COLIN Not just now. I couldn't see them then. I couldn't see anybody on the road.

OLIVER Nor could I.

PRILL When then?

COLIN I saw them this morning when I was going up to the village. They tried to grab hold of my sleeve. I thought they were gypsy kids or something.

PRILL What did you do?

COLIN I looked the other way. I was scared, so I ran for it.

PRILL Oh, what's happening to us?

OLIVER It could be hunger. If our brains are starved of nourishment it might be causing us to hallucinate.

COLIN Well let's eat then, before we go stark staring bonkers.

They go to the bags of food on the kitchen table. **Oliver** *opens Mrs O'Malley's bag. He gasps and stares.*

PRILL What's up, Olly? You've gone as white as a ghost.

COLIN Don't tell me.

OLIVER I can't believe it. Everything's covered in furry green mould. And it stinks like anything.

COLIN Well, my bread's O.K. I was just eating it. *He grabs his bag and opens it* Oh, God. Oh, no!

Colin *retches and closes the bag hurriedly. He opens the milk can and retches again.*

PRILL Put it out in the dustbin. Put it all in the dustbin — quick!

The two **boys,** *holding the bags and the can at arm's length, hurry outside.* **Prill** *stands for a moment, then quickly takes down the 'happy juice', pours it out and swallows four spoonfuls. The* **boys** *re-enter.*

COLIN No wonder Jessie's ill, Prill. Her food's crawling with maggots.

OLIVER What are you doing, Prill?

PRILL Nothing. I'm going to bed. I was awake all night.

OLIVER But what were you doing with Alison's medicine?

PRILL It's just something to help babies sleep so I thought it might help me sleep, too.

OLIVER You shouldn't **ever** do that, Prill. You should never take medicine that wasn't prescribed for you.

PRILL Oh, shut up, you stupid twit!

COLIN Leave her in peace, can't you. Let her have a sleep.

Silence. **Oliver** *looks as though he may be about to cry.*

PRILL I'm sorry, Oll. I'm just so tired, that's all.

OLIVER It's O.K.

COLIN Listen: have you noticed — food's all right when we're not in this house. Let's get some bread and cheese and apples from the village shop and we can have a picnic up at the ruined chapel. I'll take the torch, too, so I can have another look in that tunnel we climbed up, Prill.

PRILL That's a good idea. I'll come along when I wake up.

COLIN Coming, Olly?

OLIVER No. I don't think so. Not yet. I'll work on my den till Prill wakes up, then I'll come up with her.

PRILL You can't work out there in this weather, Oll.

Oliver *goes to the window.*

OLIVER It's almost stopped now.

COLIN Well, I'm going out now, before I die of hunger. I'll see you up there later on.

SCENE SEVENTEEN

Prill's bedroom. Day. **Prill** *is asleep.* **Colin** *sits on the side of the bed and shakes her till she wakes, which she does with difficulty. Sounds of digging come from outside, also the sounds of rain, occasional thunder, and a blustery wind.*

COLIN Wake up, Prill. Come on. Wake up.

PRILL   What's the matter?

COLIN   Wake up. You've been asleep all day.

Prill *sits up, bleary-eyed.*

PRILL   Is it late?

COLIN   Yes. I waited hours for you. I got soaked up there.

PRILL   Did Oliver go up?

COLIN   No. He's still digging. He was waiting for you.

PRILL   Why didn't he wake me?

COLIN   He said he tried, several times. But you were dead to the world. And he was frightened to leave you. Besides, I don't think he wanted to come out of that wretched hole. He says the rain's helped and he's made some good finds. I think he's trying to get through to Australia or something. Maybe his real parents were moles.

PRILL   I feel awful, as though I've got a mouthful of dirty socks. And I feel sick.

COLIN   You'll be all right in a minute, when you've woken up properly.

PRILL   Says you.

COLIN   Listen — I made some finds too.

PRILL   What?

COLIN   Well, one of the tombstones in the chapel cemetery is a Morrissey, dated 1751.

PRILL   So what?

COLIN   Well, Donal Morrissey came here from Donegal when he was a young man.

PRILL   So? Maybe they were ancestors.

COLIN   And another thing — the Morrisseys must have been well off then.

PRILL   Why?

COLIN   Because in those days only the rich people could have afforded gravestones. The poor had planks of wood, or were simply buried under mounds of earth.

PRILL   How do **you** know?

COLIN   Well, Oliver just told me actually.

PRILL   Hm. I knew it wasn't you talking.

COLIN   But that's not all. At one point it began pouring, so I went down the tunnel with the torch. The rain was seeping down the walls of the crack but I found this dry ledge to lie on, and I was looking at all the things carved in the rock, like, 'So-and-so loves So-and-so', and 'So-and-so rules, O.K.', and 'I love So-and-so'; but then I saw something else: this thin, spidery writing scratched into the rock — that old-fashioned sort of copperplate writing, and it said. . . I wrote it down.   **Colin** *fishes out a dirty scrap of paper from his pocket* 'C.H.M.', and, 'P.M. '48', and 'Rachel', and some others I couldn't make out. And, 'Lord have mercy', and, 'Pray for us now and in the hour of our death'. And all round the bits of writing, in a kind of frame, someone had scratched the word 'Salvation' over and over again.

The sounds of digging cease.

PRILL   What does it mean?

COLIN   I don't know. Olly says 1848 was the time of the famine.

Oliver *enters carrying his latest find.*

OLIVER   Look what I've found now.

PRILL   What is it?

OLIVER   It's a skull.

PRILL   Oh, Olly, **no.**

OLIVER   It's too small to have been an adult.

PRILL   You mean it's a **human** skull?

OLIVER   Yes. It must have been a child. But look: it's got its adult teeth — so maybe it was a child about our age.

COLIN   What are you going to do with it?

OLIVER   I think I'll take it up to show Father Hagan.

COLIN   What for?

OLIVER   I think he'd be interested. I found a place in the hole where someone had dug and filled in once before, probably a long time ago. That's where I've made most of my best finds.

COLIN   When are you going up to Father Hagan's?

OLIVER   I thought I'd go now.

COLIN   Why don't you go with him, Prill?

PRILL   But it's still raining.

COLIN   Yes but, when you didn't show up, I sort of, er. . . ate all the food I'd bought for our picnic.

PRILL   Oh, Colin. You **pig.**

COLIN   It doesn't matter. There was no point in bringing it back here was there — it would only have gone bad as soon as I brought it through the door.

PRILL   I suppose so.

COLIN   Anyway, if you go up to the village you can get something to eat and eat it before you come back.

PRILL   All right. I'll come with you, Olly. But you'd better go in the bath first.

OLIVER   Why?

PRILL   Well I'm not coming with you looking like that — plastered from head to toe in wet mud.

OLIVER   But I can't have a bath. The electricity's off. There's no hot water.

PRILL   Well at least you can clean yourself up a bit. You can have a cold wash.

OLIVER   Oh, all right.

COLIN   What happened to Aunty's clean and tidy little boy?

OLIVER   Some things are more important than keeping clean.

COLIN   You can say that again, Horatio.

PRILL   Are you coming with us, Colin?

COLIN   No. I'm full up. Anyway, I'm done in. I've walked miles today.

PRILL   Will you be all right by yourself?

COLIN   'Course I will.

PRILL   See you later then.

SCENE EIGHTEEN

Kitchen. Evening. The room is empty, lit only by candles. Sounds of a gale force wind and lashing rain from outside. We hear **Oliver** *and* **Prill** *approach at a run. They enter and slam the door behind them against the wind.*

PRILL   Thank goodness we've made it. I thought we were going to get blown away. I never thought I'd be pleased to come into this house again. I'm soaked through, and I'm frozen.

OLIVER   That's the wildest weather I've ever been out in. It was frightening, but it was exciting as well.

Oliver *and* **Prill** *take off their soaking outer clothes.* **Colin** *enters from the bedroom.*

COLIN   Oh, hi.

PRILL   Hello, Col. We're drenched.

COLIN   I can see that.

PRILL   Did you sleep?

COLIN   I've been trying. I wish I'd come with you now. Did you have anything to eat?

PRILL   Yes.

COLIN   Bring anything back?

PRILL   No. We scoffed the lot.

COLIN   I'm ravenous.

OLIVER   We'd have brought you something if we'd known.

PRILL   But it's like you said before. It wouldn't have been any good.

COLIN   Maybe. Except it's turned really cold now. Perhaps the food will be all right.

OLIVER   We can find out tomorrow.

PRILL   Have you tried the electricity?

COLIN   No.

Oliver *presses the light switch. Nothing happens.*

OLIVER   Funny. The lights were on in the village.

COLIN   Oh, that's typical, that is. They've fixed it for everyone except us.

PRILL   It was just the same with the phone. It's this **house**, I know it is.

COLIN   Anyway, it's a good job they've got a supply of candles here.

OLIVER   It would be nice to have some hot water, though, for a bath.

COLIN   And to make a cup of tea.

OLIVER   At least we've got cold water.

42

PRILL Think of all the people in the world who haven't got any water at all.

OLIVER Yes. You can live for weeks and weeks without food — but you can't survive for more than a few days without water.

COLIN Anyway, what did Father Hagan say?

OLIVER He was out.

PRILL We waited for ages but he didn't come back, so we left a message.

COLIN What did you say?

PRILL We said Mum had taken the baby to hospital in Sligo. . .

OLIVER And that I'd found a skeleton of a dog and a child's skull. . .

PRILL And that we weren't well. . .

OLIVER And could he come to see us in the morning. . .

PRILL And could he ask a vet to come to look at Jessie.

COLIN Oh, good. He should be down in the morning then.

PRILL Yes. Let's hope he fetches a vet too.

COLIN Poor Jessie's like a bag of bones. She can't even stand up any more.

Pause.

PRILL Well at least we should be able to sleep tonight. That heat's gone and there's no baby to scream all night.

OLIVER I'm going to bed now. I'm worn to a frazzle.

COLIN Don't say words like 'frazzle'. It makes me think of bacon.

PRILL I'm going too. What about you, Colin?

COLIN In a minute. I'll just try the phone. *He picks up the receiver, pulls a face and slams the phone down* Nothing. I'm so hungry I'll never be able to sleep. I must eat something.

PRILL There's nothing here.

COLIN I wonder if humans could eat dog biscuits?

PRILL Oh, Colin!

OLIVER I don't see why not. We're only animals, mammals, the same as they are. If dog food had poison in it, it would poison dogs, wouldn't it?

Colin *gets a packet of dog biscuits out of the cupboard. He tips a biscuit into his hand and studies it.*

COLIN Shall I?

PRILL No, Col.

OLIVER It's up to you.

Colin *puts it into his mouth and begins to chew. He finds it difficult to swallow. He goes to the sink and gets a mug of water and tries to help wash it down with that.*

OLIVER What's it like?

PRILL Don't encourage him.

COLIN You can't swallow it. It's like having a mouthful of gravel. *He rinses the rest from his mouth and spits it into the sink* I've got to have something though — or I'll die of hunger before morning.

PRILL 'Course you won't.

COLIN I **will**. And anyway these hunger pains will keep me awake all night. I was awake all last night as it is. I don't think I could survive another sleepless night without going round the bend. *He goes to the fridge and after peering in, brings out an opened, half-full tin of dog meat which has a spoon sticking up out of it.*

PRILL Colin! You're not going to eat that!

COLIN Well it's not as chewy as the biscuit. It's only meat. Look — it says so on the label. *He sniffs it* Smells all right.

PRILL No, Colin!

Colin *takes a spoonful of dog meat, inspects it, then puts it into his mouth and drops the spoon back into the tin. He begins to chew, then gags, runs to the sink and throws up, gasping, gulping water from the tap. Then* **Prill** *begins to scream.*

OLIVER What's the matter, Prill? What's the matter?

PRILL Look! Look! The spoon! The spoon in the dog meat! Look at all the maggots crawling up the handle!

Oliver *is aghast,* **Colin** *vomits again,* **Prill** *screams.*

SCENE NINETEEN

The boy's bedroom. Night. **Colin** *and* **Oliver** *sleep restlessly.*
Oliver *begins to thrash about. By each boy's bed there is a
candle burning in a jam jar. We hear the sounds of a* **Baby**
crying and the storm raging unabated. **Oliver** *sits up suddenly,
struggling, shouting out for* **Colin.**

OLIVER   Colin! Colin! Colin!   *The last 'Colin' becomes a
long scream.*

COLIN   *sitting up*   What's the matter?   *Urgently*   What is
it?

OLIVER   Colin! Help me!

Colin *jumps out of his bed and sits on the side of* **Oliver's.**
Colin *tries to hold* **Oliver** *still and calm him.*

COLIN   It's all right, Olly. I'm here. It's me, Colin. What's
the matter? It's just a dream.

OLIVER   Oh, Colin.   *He goes limp*   I was having a dream.

COLIN   What about?

OLIVER   *still distressed*   I can't remember the beginning —
it went on for a long time and it was very complicated. But at
the end I was at the bottom of a deep pit with lots of other
people and our arms and legs were all tangled up, and it was
raining on us.

COLIN   You probably heard the rain in your sleep. And it's
like you said before — you were probably thinking about
your den, and finding the skull and everything.

OLIVER   But then someone started shovelling wet earth on
us and it was going in my eyes and mouth, and I shouted out,
'Please let us out! Don't bury us yet! Some of us are still
alive!' But this man just went on smiling and shovelling — I
think it was Father Hagan. I said, '**Please** let us out! Some of
us are **not** dead!' and everyone was screaming. And then
only the baby was left alive — crying and crying.

COLIN   Hey! You **weren't** dreaming that. Listen.

Colin *and* **Oliver** *listen together to the* **Baby's** *cries.*

COLIN   There really **is** a baby crying.

OLIVER   Aunty Jeannie and Alison must have come back
while we've been asleep.

COLIN   Let's go and see.

As **Colin** *and* **Oliver** *get up from the bed,* **Prill,** *in the next room, screams a spine-chilling scream.*

SCENE TWENTY

Prill's bedroom. Night. A candle burns beside the bed. **Prill,** *sobbing, is staring out of the open window despite the wind and rain. The gale rages — the* **Baby's** *cries can be heard louder or softer as the noise of the wind varies.* **Colin** *enters and tries to close the window.* **Prill** *struggles to prevent him.*

PRILL   Don't! Don't! We won't be able to breathe if you do that.

COLIN   Stop it, Prill! You're soaked!

PRILL   Don't, Colin! Don't. Oh, **please**! How can we get out now!

COLIN   Calm down, Prill. It's all right. Really it is.

Prill *gives up the struggle and bursts into tears.* **Colin** *slams the window shut and cuddles* **Prill.** *The sounds of the* **Baby** *and the storm continue from outside.* **Oliver** *enters carrying his candle.*

OLIVER   There's nobody here.

COLIN   There must be.

OLIVER   I've looked everywhere.

COLIN   But the baby?

OLIVER   It must be outside. Or. . .

COLIN   Or what?

OLIVER   Why don't they comfort her? If only someone would comfort her!

Prill's *sobs are subsiding. The* **boys** *get her to sit down and sit one each side of her on her bed and put an arm round her. The* **Baby's** *cries are joined by the weak moaning of two older* **children.**

PRILL   Listen! Can you hear it?

Pause, as they sit quietly, terrified, listening.

COLIN   We won't stay here, Prill. We'll go and stay in the village. We'll leave as soon as it gets light.

46

OLIVER   No. We'll go **now**. Look: there's a light burning in Donal's caravan.

COLIN   He's probably asleep.

OLIVER   No. Old people don't need much sleep.

COLIN   How do you know?

OLIVER   He's awake. I **know**. He's waiting for us.

PRILL   I'm not going **there**.

OLIVER   Yes. We must. We can't stay here.

PRILL   Not to that nasty old man.

OLIVER   Prill! We must get away from this house. Come **on!** **Trust** me, Prill!

Colin and **Oliver** pull **Prill** to her feet.

OLIVER   Get dressed!

COLIN   Olly's right, Prill. Come on.

OLIVER   Just put your coat on over your pyjamas.

PRILL   What about Jessie? We can't leave her.

COLIN   She's too weak to walk.

PRILL   I'll carry her.

OLIVER   No! We'll get the taxi to take her to the vet first thing in the morning. **We must go now!**

Day Six
SCENE TWENTY-ONE

Donal's caravan. Early morning. The first hint of dawn shows through the caravan windows, and it grows lighter as the scene continues. The electric light is on. The sound of the gale can be heard outside but it dwindles as the day approaches. **Donal** *is sitting beside his table. The caravan is dirty and crammed with the collected paraphernalia of an old man. We hear the three children approach and their knock on the door.*

DONAL   *without moving*   Come in.

Colin, Prill and **Oliver** *enter, wet and windblown and frightened.*

DONAL   *sharply*   Close the door. Sit by the stove and get warm. There's blankets there.

Donal *points to three old, smelly blankets.* **Oliver** *fetches them and gives one each to* **Colin** *and* **Prill** *who sit on the floor close to the stove.*

DONAL   Dish up some stew, boy. It's on the stove.

Oliver *dishes out three bowlfuls and hands them round, but instead of starting on his own he puts his hand into his anorak pocket and produces two envelopes which he passes to* **Donal.**

OLIVER   These are for you. They're the best of my finds.

Donal *accepts them and takes out from the first a small, round, metal object about the size of a walnut, fixed onto a piece of rotten wood.* **Donal** *looks astonished, glances intently at* **Oliver,** *looks back at his gift, shakes it — it rattles — and smiles.*

OLIVER   I tried to clean it. I think it might be silver. There's an initial on it, look. An 'M'.

Donal *is very affected. He opens the second envelope and removes carefully from it a scrap of purply-red material about 5cm square.*

OLIVER   There was more of it — but it crumbled away when I touched it. There were bits of wood too. Maybe everything had been in a box.

Donal *stares at these things for a long time, while the children greedily gulp the stew, and then he lays them carefully on the table.*

DONAL   Where did you find these things?

OLIVER   Where I've been digging. I began making a den. It's just at the side of the bungalow.

DONAL   *pointing to the material and talking dreamily, almost as if to himself*   Cost money that would.   It's silk. Otherwise it would have rotted, surely. Oh, they were fine folk.

COLIN   Who were?

OLIVER   The silver thing's a baby's rattle. The handle's missing — but that's what it is.

DONAL   Pass me that box, boy.

On one of Donal's stacks of belongings is a box less dusty than the rest because of frequent handling. **Oliver** *fetches it.*

OLIVER   Is this your treasure box, Mr Morrissey?

DONAL   Yes. Look.

Opening it, **Donal** *takes out a baby's rattle, a tattered square of dark red silk, and a shabby black prayer book. He holds out the rattle for* **Oliver** *to see.*

DONAL   Like the one you found, but perfect. The handle is of apple wood and there's a design of leaves carved on it. The top is silver, as you said, and the 'M' is engraved there. And these two pieces of silk must have come from the same thing — probably a shawl. These were hers. All she'd got left from those days. And this was her prayer book.

PRILL   Whose? Your mother's?

OLIVER   His **grandmother's.** Bridget Morrissey. She was born here but went away to live in Donegal when she was married.

Donal *opens the prayer book and shows the inscription inside.*

DONAL   See that: 'Bridget Morrissey. Ballimagliesh, 1865.' She was seventeen when she wrote that. It's a fine hand so it is. They could all read and write. This is over a hundred years old. But these. . . these are older still. Much older.

OLIVER   And you lived with her in Donegal — before you came here?

DONAL   So I did. All her children went away — or were sent away for stealing food to feed their families — England, Canada, America, Australia. She never heard from them. My mother was the last to go — I never knew who my father was. I grew up with my grandmother — till she died and they wouldn't give me the tenancy of the farm. Then I was homeless. So I came back here, where she had lived until she married. The Morrisseys were always Ballimagliesh people. Wealthy too, in the old days, before the English came and took our land — made us tenants and labourers on land that was rightfully ours. There are Morrisseys buried in the Chapel of Our Lady, above Ballimagliesh Strand.

COLIN   I know. I found a headstone in the ruins. It had Morrissey on it. And I found some names and things carved in rock in a tunnel there.

DONAL   *alert and interested*   Oh, yes. You've been down the tunnel then? It was **her** told me about that — before she died. That was the first thing I did when I came here — went to look for those names in that hiding place by the Strand.

COLIN   And they were your family?

DONAL   *in a dream-like voice of great passion*   To be sure, poor souls. No rest for them. No refuge. No one to bury them. All perished.

OLIVER   They died in the famine, didn't they.

DONAL   All of them, except Bridget. All the Morrisseys. And no one to bury them. Others were thrown into pits of lime, dozens together, like animals.

PRILL   You mean in the 1840s?

DONAL   Yes. In the Great Hunger.

Silence.

Oliver *goes to* **Donal** *and puts a hand on his shoulder. The old man is startled for a second, and then he lays a hand on* **Oliver's.**

OLIVER   There's one thing I don't understand. Your grandmother — she was born in 1848. I mean, if she was seventeen in 1865, that means she must have been born in 1848. So she was just born when the rest of the family were dying?

It is now light. There is the sound of approaching footsteps and a knock at the door.

DONAL   Who is it?

FATHER HAGAN   *off stage*   Father Hagan, Donal.

DONAL   Come in, come in, do.

Father Hagan *enters and sees the children.*

FATHER HAGAN   Thanks be to God you're all safe.

OLIVER   Hello, Father Hagan. ⎫
COLIN   Hello.   ⎬   *Together.*
PRILL   Hello, Father.   ⎭

DONAL   Come in, Father. You're a stranger surely.

FATHER HAGAN   It's only two days, Donal. And in fact I'm not really visiting you now. I got back very late last night and found a note from these children, so I came down at first light. The house was deserted, but the dog's still there so I knew they wouldn't be far. I just called to see if you knew where they were.

DONAL   I do indeed. My young friends are paying a lonely old man an early morning visit. Look.   *He indicates* **Oliver's** *'finds'.*

SCENE TWENTY-TWO

Kitchen. Day. **Father Hagan, Colin, Prill** *and* **Oliver** *sit at the table drinking tea.*

FATHER HAGAN   What Oliver has found here was probably their last hiding place.

OLIVER   It was just a big hole roofed over with twigs and stuff.

FATHER HAGAN   It's hard to believe some of the tales about the famine years, but what happened to the Morrissey's wasn't unusual.

PRILL   What **did** happen to them?

FATHER HAGAN   Well, at that time, they would have worked as labourers on the landlord's land — land which had once been their own. They would have been paid, of course, but their earnings were small and had to be repaid to the landlord as rent for their cottage and for the little plot of land on which they grew potatoes.

OLIVER   The potatoes they grew were all the poor had to live on.

FATHER HAGAN   In better years they might have had a few hens or a pig.

OLIVER   The famine years were good years, weren't they, for all crops except potatoes.

FATHER HAGAN   Yes indeed. Wet springs and hot summers — very much like this year, in fact — ideal conditions for potato blight. The English landlords grew rich exporting food under armed guard while the poor died of starvation. People killed off their dogs and ate them. Some people ate rats.

OLIVER   Some even fed on the bodies of those that had died. It was a kind of cannibalism.

FATHER HAGAN   Possibly, possibly.   *He gives* **Oliver** *a 'look'*   But I don't think there was a lot of that.

COLIN   There couldn't have been much meat on the bodies if they'd died of starvation.

FATHER HAGAN   Starvation and disease. When people are seriously malnourished they are at the mercy of every illness, and epidemics spread like wildfire.

OLIVER   There were so many bodies, lots remained unburied, or were thrown into great pits — mass graves — and covered with lime.

FATHER HAGAN   That's quite right, Oliver. And they say the children came to look like monkeys, wizened and covered with hair; and they lost their powers of speech. In the end they could only open and close their mouths but no sound came through. The potato fields turned black with the blight — they looked as though fire had passed over them. And during those hot summers, the awful stench of rotting potatoes hung over everything. The entire potato harvest was destroyed almost overnight, for several years running. Imagine it. The plants above the ground turned black, and the potatoes themselves in the earth became nothing but skins of black stinking slime.

Pause.

PRILL   What about the Morrisseys?

FATHER HAGAN   They were a small family for those days. Five children. But the fifth was no sooner born than the one-year-old died. The story goes that the mother took the corpse and left it in the town; she stole a loaf of bread and left the dead child instead of money. It was all she had to give.

PRILL   I saw her.

FATHER HAGAN   Yes.

PRILL   But she looked so old.

FATHER HAGAN   What she lived through aged her.

PRILL   And then?

FATHER HAGAN   There were three older children — about your ages when they. . . at the end, and a baby girl. They were evicted. The English landlord had them driven out of their home because they couldn't pay the rent — and he wanted the land for sheep.

PRILL   Where did they live?

FATHER HAGAN   It would only have been a mud cabin with a thatched roof; and it stood here — on the site of this house.

Colin *and* **Prill** *exchange looks of dawning comprehension.*

PRILL   So it happened to us because we were **here**. On the very spot where they lived?

OLIVER   And died.

FATHER HAGAN   Yes. They were never properly buried, and I suppose Oliver. . . released them, in a manner of speaking.

PRILL   By digging his hole.

COLIN   But how come they died **here**, if they'd been driven away?

FATHER HAGAN   When they were evicted the house would have been destroyed — the roof burned, the walls demolished. Then the Morrisseys took shelter in. . .

COLIN   That crack in the rock up by the chapel.

FATHER HAGAN   That's right. But then, after a while, they must have crept back to the ruins of their home and dug themselves a hole to live in — a scalpeen it was called.

COLIN   Out where Oliver was digging?

OLIVER   Yes. And they died in it.

PRILL   All of them?

OLIVER   All of them — except for the baby.

FATHER HAGAN   Someone found the baby among the corpses — heard it crying. It was given to another poor family who had managed to survive. The scalpeen was filled in, with the bodies still there.

OLIVER   The bodies of the family and their dog.

FATHER HAGAN   So it seems.

OLIVER   And the skull is of one of the children.

FATHER HAGAN   Probably. The workmen will be down soon to complete the excavation that you began. Whatever human remains are found will be given a proper burial up at the chapel.

PRILL   And the baby was Bridget?

FATHER HAGAN   Yes. Bridget. Donal's grandmother. She married a cousin, Michael Morrissey, and they went to farm in Donegal.

PRILL   So it was **her** voice we heard — the baby crying in the night.

53

FATHER HAGAN   Yes.   *Pause.* **Colin** *and* **Prill** *exchange looks: everything is becoming clear now*   Once the men have finished their work here, the Morrissey's agony will be over at last.

They hear the sound of a car approaching.

COLIN   Listen — someone's coming.

FATHER HAGAN   That'll be the vet coming to see your dog.

PRILL   She already seems a little better this morning.

The phone rings, making them all jump.

PRILL   *excitedly*   **The phone's on!**

Prill *and* **Colin** *jump up and run to the phone, bumping into each other.* **Prill** *gets there first.*

PRILL   *into the phone*   Yes. . . Yes. . . Oh. . . Really. . . Good. . . That's marvellous. . . Yes. . . Yes. . . Bye.

Prill *drops the phone onto its cradle and beams.*

PRILL   That was Mum. She says Alison's better already. And Dad's at the hospital with her. They're coming this afternoon.

Colin, Prill *and* **Oliver** *jump and whoop for joy.* **Father Hagan** *looks on.*

THE END

STAGING THE PLAY

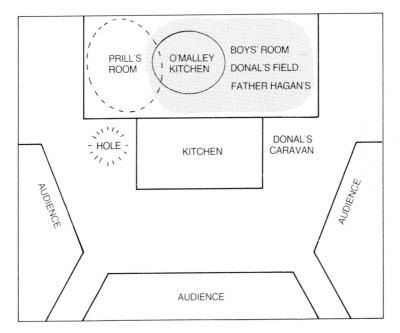

Your school   will probably have a proscenium stage and enough blocks to build a slightly lower acting area out into the auditorium. This gives a basic 'thrust' stage which will probably be the most useful for this play which requires a number of interiors. You could try to use a central space for acting 'in the round', but as most of the action takes place in kitchens and bedrooms, and as these places are best suggested by fairly large pieces of furniture, you would slow down the action considerably with scene shifting.

It would be a good idea to set a bed permanently in Prill's room, which is used quite often and to make some effort with a family dining area for the kitchen which is used most of all. Oliver's hole and Donal's caravan can be set on the floor of the auditorium. You could use sacking to cover the front of the stage for the hole. This could be daubed with mud and a scattering of sand and leaves on the floor might be effective. Don't try to roof the hole, though, or you'll have problems with lighting.

The rest of the set should be kept flexible. If you place a smallish table in Prill's room — towards centre stage — it could become a part of the O'Malley kitchen by the simple addition of a checked cloth. Actors positioning themselves for a scene in this multi-location space should carry on their own chairs and hand props where appropriate. This same space could also represent Donal's field. If you have a cyclorama, a flood of green turning to red could represent the field burning. Try to suggest a place by the use of one simple prop — a screen with a holy picture on it, for example, is both easy to set and would help create Father Hagan's home.

If each area can be lit separately the change from scene to scene will be smooth and simple. At the end of a scene, lights should fade on the area of action, actors should move to their next positions and the lights can then be brought up on them once they are in place. You may be able to use special effects too — sidelighting can be creepy, as can the use of coloured light.

Keep props and scenery to a minimum. Create mood and place with as few pieces of furniture as you can. The less you have, the less there is to go wrong!

Remember that a script is a skeleton, not a finished product. If lines don't seem to work in performance they can always be changed or cut. These ideas on staging are not the only possibilities either — everyone's ideas are worth a try until you discover what works best for your group in the space you have available.

WORK ON AND AROUND THE SCRIPT

Drama

1 Work in a group of four or five. Decide among yourselves which are the key moments or incidents in the play and choose three of these. Using as many people from your group as necessary, create a tableau or 'picture' to show exactly what is happening.

Show your frozen pictures to the rest of the class, and ask them to provide a title for each 'picture'.

2 Throughout the play Oliver seems to be a bit of an outsider. From what we learn of his parents, they appear rather overprotective and anxious.

Work in a group of two or three. One of you is Mrs Blakeman, who wants to invite Oliver on holiday with her family. The other(s) are Oliver's parents.

How does Mrs Blakeman persuade them to allow Oliver to go away on holiday?

3 In country areas, people tend to be very interested in the activities of their neighbours, and especially new arrivals to the district.

Work with a partner. One of you is a rather inquisitive neighbour who is visiting Mrs O'Malley, and is eager to hear all about the family from England staying in the new house, who seem to be having problems. The other is Mrs O'Malley, who does not approve of gossip. How does the conversation develop? Can Mrs O'Malley continue the conversation without offending her neighbour?

4 In the play all three children have recurrent nightmares. Work in a small group, and take turns to describe the worst nightmare you have ever had.

Choose the nightmare which seems the most terrifying and

act it out, using as many of the group as necessary. Remember that sounds and movements in dreams can seem exaggerated. Try to create the atmosphere of horror which the children experienced in the play.

5 Work with a partner. Imagine that you are either Colin or Prill, and you have managed to speak to your father briefly on the telephone in the local village. You want to convey to your father that things are not going well, but at the same time you don't want to make him unnecessarily worried.

One of you should take on the role of Mr Blakeman. He is eager to believe that his family are having a wonderful holiday, and brushes aside any hints of trouble. Carry on the telephone conversation.

6 Mrs Blakeman must have been very relieved to get Alison, her sick baby, to the hospital, even though it meant leaving the other children alone.

Work in a group of two or three. One of you is Mrs Blakeman. The others are members of the hospital staff, who are puzzled and worried by the strange, starving condition of the baby. What questions can they ask to discover an explanation for the baby's condition? How can they find out what's been happening without upsetting Mrs Blakeman any further?

7 Work in groups of three. Act out the scene in which Colin takes Prill and Oliver to the cave. Imagine what the cave is like. Is it very dark and eery? How do you feel as you look at the inscriptions carved over a century ago? Do you find any other clues about what happened there?

8 Work in pairs. Rumours about the strange events in the neighbourhood have become widespread. One of you is a reporter from a local newspaper who is investigating the story of ghosts and hallucinations. Your partner is either Colin, Prill or Oliver.

What kinds of questions will the journalist ask? Will these questions show whether the journalist believes in ghosts, or regards the whole story as a joke?

9 Work in a group of four or five. A TV or radio documentary is being made about the strange happenings in Ballymagliesh, and the links with victims of the famine. With your group create the programme. Decide what kind of historical background you will need to include, which of the family and local people you will want to interview, and what kind of sound effects and visuals to use. If you have access to a tape-recorder or video camera you may be able to produce the actual documentary programme.

10   Sometimes hauntings are investigated scientifically. Tape-recorders, thermometers (to record any dramatic drops in temperature or to discover 'cold spots') and cameras are used to try to establish whether or not a place is haunted.

Work in a small group. You are investigating the events in Ballymagliesh. What evidence can you find to support the stories told by the children? If you spent a night in the holiday house what might you see and hear? What kind of dreams might you have?

Each group should report its findings in as 'scientific' a way as possible to the rest of the class, who are meeting as members of the Society for Psychical Research. Your teacher could take on the role of President of the Society.

Written Work
1   Make a list of all the different incidents which caused the children to feel that something was wrong.

Could you find natural explanations for any of these?

Which would you have found the most frightening? Compare your list with those of others in the class.

2   Imagine that you are either Prill or Colin. Write diary entries for the first few days of the holiday. What kinds of thing will you include in each entry?

3   Oliver is a very serious, studious boy. Colin complains that he always has his head in a book, and finds it difficult to be friendly.

Write a school report for Oliver, as if you were his form teacher. Try to include remarks about as many aspects of his behaviour at school as you can.

4   Imagine you are either Colin or Prill. Write a letter to a friend in England in which you describe your holiday house and the surrounding area. Include a description of Oliver and your feelings about him. Try to include some positive as well as negative comments.

5 In the play, both Donal and Oliver are outsiders although in different ways. Oliver's origins and family history are quite mysterious. Is it possible that he somehow has a special link with the Morrisseys, or is he someone who is especially sensitive to atmosphere? Invent a family history and a family tree for Oliver which will fill in his background before he was adopted.

6 Assuming that Oliver has a special gift for tuning in to the spirit of a place, write a further episode in his life in which he is once again involved in strange happenings.

7 Donal lives alone, wrapped up in the tragic history of his family. He resents the intrusion of the family holidaying in the bungalow. Imagine that you are Donal sitting in your caravan one evening, looking at the relics of your family. Write a poem or a monologue expressing your thoughts and feelings about the past and the present.

If you choose to write a monologue, remember that it must be designed to be heard, not only read in print. This will affect the style of your writing, and the sentence structure. Share your poem or your monologue with the rest of the class.

8 The condition of the Blakeman baby, Alison, may have caused concern in the hospital to which she was taken. As a member of the medical staff — a doctor or nurse who was on duty when she was admitted — write a report on Alison's condition, and include any explanations for it which seem plausible.

9 Write a newspaper report of the events in Ballymagliesh. Try to make your headlines as intriguing as possible.

10 Imagine that the owner of the bungalow wants to sell it because of what has happened there. Write a description of the house and grounds as if you are the house agent who has the job of selling it. Which features will you want to emphasise, and which will you want to play down?

FROM NOVEL TO PLAY

The play, *Black Harvest*, has been rewritten from a novel of the same name. One of the most disturbing scenes in the novel — the hallucination in the shop — has not been included in the script, although we do hear Prill telling Father O'Hagan what happened.

Read the following extract from the novel.

The shop was gloomy and full of people waiting. Prill edged past them trying to make out what was on the shelves. Why was it so dark inside? There was hardly enough light to read her mother's shopping list. Then she remembered, there was a power cut in Ballimagliesh. They were doing some maintenance work, Mrs O'Malley had told her. That would be why they'd rigged up this smelly oil-lamp that smoked and spluttered over her head.

When a wave of fresh customers came in Prill was pushed to one side. People jostled each other and tried to get to the front of the queue. But it was strangely quiet. All she could hear was money chinking and things being slid across the counter. The shop was so crowded she couldn't raise her arm to hold the list under the lamp. When her turn came she'd give it to the shopkeeper, that would be quickest. She wanted to get out really, she could hardly breathe in this stuffy place.

The shop door rattled again and Prill glanced back. Her heart warmed to see the fat face of a clergyman. It just had to be that Father Hagan. Oliver was right, he was a bit like Friar Tuck. She smiled at him. But he had already turned his back to talk to someone. She just caught the words 'tobacco', 'very difficult' and 'old Donal'. Then she heard something else. An argument was going on at the counter. The general mumbling in the queue died away and everyone leaned forward to listen.

But the customer clearly didn't want anybody to hear. Prill could only make out the tone of the voice, the note of pleading. Then she heard, 'Give me what you have then,' from the shopkeeper. 'We've got little enough ourselves, God knows.' And suddenly, very close, she could see a hand thrust out at him, with the fingers drawn up tightly over the palm, shrivelled yellowing fingers like turkey claws.

It lay lifelessly on the bare counter and Prill watched the plump, pink hand of the man prise the fingers open slowly, one by one, revealing nothing.

'I'm sorry, but if you have no money at all . . .' then the words turned into mumbling again. The woman's voice deadened into a low, monotonous keening. It was the most desolate sound Prill had ever heard.

Suddenly there was a shriek. 'For the love of God, spare me *something*!' Then several things happened at once. The shop door blew shut with a bang and buckets rolled over the floor. Prill heard Father Hagan wheezing at the back, helping another man stack them up again and laughing. A strip light over the counter was flickering into life and the tubby, white-overalled shopkeeper blinked up at it. In that instant the shawled figure at the counter leaned forward and grabbed.

A neat pyramid of loaves, buns and cakes toppled over. 'Take what I have, and may God help me,' the woman cried shrilly and, pulling a bundle from under her arm, she thrust it at the goggling shop owner.

As she pushed past, Prill could smell the new loaf in her hand. The swinging oil-lamp turned the woman's face a muddy yellow and patched the shrunken face with shadow. The girl saw the familiar domed head, the remains of springy, russet hair, the gaunt cheekbones almost breaking the flesh.

All the lights were back on in the shop and the man was reading her list and saying pleasantly, 'I'll get you a little box for this surely. Oh, you've got a bag? If you'll give it to me then. The bacon's out at the back, I won't be a minute.'

As she waited, Prill fingered the sacking bundle lightly, then laid her whole hand flat upon it. A coldness came up through the coarse webbing. She pushed at it. The lump inside was heavy, unyielding, and gave off a high, gamey smell.

Her fingers crept to the end of the sacking where the loose brown folds had fallen open. She could hear the bacon-slicer whining faintly in the back room, and Father Hagan chatting away somewhere behind her. She didn't want to unwrap the bundle, she wanted to run out of the shop. But something compelled her to roll the thing over and over on the counter till the sacking fell away, and with it the layer of filthy rags underneath. Then she could see properly.

The smell coming out of the bundle was like very bad meat. But what Prill saw, lying on the counter, was a human child. The tiny body was naked, the face blotched and swollen, the eyes glazed in a white, expressionless stare like a fish on a slab. It looked like Alison.

She remembered the shopkeeper coming back with the bacon and staring at her open-mouthed as she stood clutching the countertop, staring down at the dead baby, screaming the one word 'No!' over and over again. She remembered him scuttling into the back shouting for his wife, 'Maraid! Maraid! Come here for God's sake!' Then a sick darkness wrapped itself round her as she plunged about on the shop floor, knocking into displays of pans and glasses when she crashed to the ground.

She remembered getting outside and being sick against a mossy, white-washed wall, and Father Hagan peering down at her anxiously as the blood from a cut on her head streamed down her face, like warm rain.

1 Why do you think that Nigel Gray decided not to include this scene directly in his script?

2 Working in a small group, try to stage the scene. You may want to script it, writing down the dialogue as it appears in the extract. You may need to invent extra dialogue for bystanders and for the people in the shop. How will you create the strange atmosphere?

3 Work with a partner.
One of you was in the shop when Prill had her strange experience. Your partner is a friend who was not present. Describe everything that you saw. Can you find any explanation for what took place?

4 Work with a partner or in a group of three.
Prill was obviously very upset by what happened. If you were with her when she recovered consciousness, how would you help her to calm down? Could you find a way to get her to describe what she saw?

5 Imagine you are the woman who at the height of the famine abandons her dead baby in the shop. Write a short poem in which you speak your thoughts about your sufferings.

THE GREAT HUNGER
1845–1851

In the nineteenth century, Ireland was ruled directly from London by the British Parliament. The majority of the Irish people lived on a few acres of land and depended entirely on their yearly crop of potatoes. One or two acres of land could produce enough potatoes to feed a family of five or six for a year. The ease with which the potato could be cultivated and its high yield, were responsible for the large population, the high rents and the frantic subdivision of land. Most people did not own their land and because the land was often sublet, they had no security of tenure. If they failed to pay the high rents demanded by their landlords, they could be evicted from their homes and turned out on the roads to beg or starve. The possession of a piece of land literally made the difference between life and death for the mass of the poverty-stricken and oppressed population.

Although the potato was easily grown and provided a nutritious diet, it was dangerous to rely on one crop to support the entire population. Potatoes did not keep and could not be stored. More importantly, the crop was liable to frequent failure, and when it failed, as it did several times in the 1830s, there was no substitute food for the majority of people. In 1844 a report was received from America of an unknown disease which had attacked the crops there. This disease was potato blight, and in 1845 this dreadful blight attacked the Irish potato crop. A good harvest had been expected, but the potato plants rotted in the fields, which turned black overnight. Below ground, the potatoes became a stinking, putrid mass. The potato crop of 1846 was an almost total failure. In 1847 the blight was less severe but people had eaten their seed potatoes so the overall crop was again small. With further crop failures, it was not until 1851 that the famine seemed to be largely over.

Government Intervention

The Corn Laws were repealed in 1846 allowing free trade in corn and food. But the plentiful and cheap supplies that were expected from Canada and America did not actually arrive until the 1870s. It was widely believed that free market forces would adjust economic problems without the government intervention that was so necessary if the disaster was to be overcome. Cheap food would be provided, but the people must earn the money to pay for it. Throughout the famine years, when Britain also suffered from a shortage of food, Ireland continued to export wheat, barley, cattle, sheep and pigs, because the Irish economy was so tied to the needs of Britain.

A programme of road building and other public works had been started in some parts of Ireland in order to create jobs, but it began too late and there was not enough work to go round. Pay was often held up and sometimes wages were never paid. While many private individuals and religious organisations did what they could to help, these efforts were powerless against the scale of the tragedy.

Evictions

Some landlords gave food and money to their tenants, but others evicted those who could no longer pay their rents.

This is a description of an eviction in County Galway:

It was the most appalling sight I ever witnessed: women, young and old, running wildly to and fro with small portions of their property to save it from the wreck — the screaming of the children, and the wild wailings of the mothers driven from home and shelter. . .In the first instance the roofs and portions of the walls only were thrown down. But that Friday night the wretched creatures pitched a few poles slant-wise against the walls covering them with thatch in order to provide shelter for the night. When this was perceived, the next day the bailiffs were despatched with orders to pull down all the walls and root up the foundations in order to prevent the poor people from daring to take shelter amid the ruins.

An eviction. Tenants are dragged out with the help of troops and the 'tumbling' of the houses begins. *Illustrated London News*, 16 December 1848

Starvation

The winter of 1846–47 was exceptionally severe. People already weakened by hunger had no resistance to disease and began to die in great numbers, the children in particular. It was the labourer and cottier classes and the small farmers, especially in the counties in the South and West, who suffered most.

A magistrate visited Skibbereen, a village near Cork, and this account was published in *The Times* on Christmas Eve 1846:

> I was surprised to find the wretched hamlet apparently deserted. I entered some of the hovels and the scenes which presented themselves were such as no pen or tongue can convey the slightest idea of. In the first, six famished and ghastly skeletons, to all appearances dead, were huddled in a corner on some filthy straw, their sole covering which seemed a ragged horsecloth, their wretched legs hanging about, naked above the

Famine funeral at Skibbereen. Coffins were unprocurable. *Illustrated London News*, 30 January 1847

knees. I approached with horror, and found by a low moaning they were alive — they were in fever, four children, a woman and what had once been a man. It is impossible to go through the detail. Suffice it to say, that in a few minutes I was surrounded by at least 200 such phantoms. . . I found myself grasped by a woman with an infant just born in her arms and the remains of a filthy sack across her loins — the sole covering of herself and the baby. The same morning the police opened a house on the adjoining lands, which was observed shut for many days, and two dead corpses were found, lying upon the mud floor, half devoured by rats.

In that area of Cork, deaths were so numerous that 'coffins could not be had for half of those who expired from want. . .so that in many places the deceased are tied up in straw.' Thousands died from starvation and more often, from the diseases like typhus and cholera that followed.

Fearing the Irish would become lazy and dependent on the cheap food the government had been providing, all government aid to Ireland was stopped in 1847.

Emigration

With only the prospect of starvation and death if they stayed, people began to leave Ireland. Some went to England, but by far the largest number emigrated to the United States and Canada. In some cases the landlords themselves paid their tenants' fares. However, as conditions on board the crowded ships were so bad, many died on the journey. In Quebec, where thousands went, one eye-witness described how 'hundreds were literally flung on the beach, left amid the mud and stones to crawl on dry land as they could.'

Gross Isle, the immigration sickness centre in the St Lawrence River at Quebec, saw the worst of the horrors when the ships arrived with their cargos of sick and dying immigrants. A monument was placed on the island by the doctors. The inscription on it reads:

> 'In this secluded spot lie the mortal remains of 5294 persons, who flying from pestilence and famine in Ireland in the year 1847 found in America but a grave.'

In 1848 when the potato crop failed again, evictions increased, public works were stopped, and disease was rife. 1849 was the most terrible year of all and yet food continued to be exported from Ireland — food which the starving people had no money to buy. In February 1849, a ball was held by the Lady Mayoress at the Mansion House in Dublin at which 'refreshments of a most récherché description were supplied with inexhaustible profusion.'

Out of a population of about eight million, at least a million died from starvation and disease in the Famine years, and in the ten years from 1845, two million (a *quarter* of the population) emigrated. Not surprisingly, the Famine left behind a legacy of hatred and resentment.

Drama

1 Work with a partner. One of you is an old person who has survived the Famine. Many years have passed since then, and you are telling a young friend or relation what it was like to live then. What do you remember most vividly? Who do you blame for the disaster?

A 'scalpeen' at Dunmore. Evicted tenants roof a hole with furze in the 'tumbled' village. *Illustrated London News*, 22 December 1849

2 Read the description of an eviction, and look carefully at the picture on pages 66–67. Work with a partner. One of you has been to Ireland and has seen an eviction. The other is a friend in England, who finds it hard to believe that such poverty and misery exists. What details will you use to convince your.friend of the truth of what you say?

3 Create a tableau (a frozen picure) of an eviction, basing your work on the pictures in this section. Ask each person in your tableau to speak his or her thoughts aloud.

4 Work in a group. (It may need to be quite large to try out this scene.) One of you is a landlord who dreams he has died and is awaiting judgement for his crimes. Scenes of suffering from the Famine and its aftermath are replayed before him, as his former tenants rise up to accuse him. Their voices might speak out against him, one after another. You could appoint a ghostly prosecutor, and a judge. How is the landlord's fate decided? What is his punishment?

During the whole of a dull, dark, and soundless day in the autumn of the year, when the clouds hung oppressively low in the heavens, I had been passing alone, on horseback, through a singularly dreary tract of country, and at length found myself, as the shades of evening drew on, within view of the melancholy House of Usher. I know not how it was—but, with the first glimpse of the building, a sense of insufferable gloom pervaded my spirit. I say unsufferable; for the feeling was unrelieved by any of that half-pleasurable, because poetic, sentiment, with which the mind usually receives even the sternest natural images of the desolate or terrible. I looked upon the scene before me—upon the mere house, and the simple landscape features of the domain—upon the bleak walls—upon the vacant eye-like windows—upon a few rank sedges—and upon a few white trunks of decayed trees—with an utter depression of soul which I can compare to no earthly sensation more properly than to the after-dream of the reveller upon opium—the bitter lapse into every-day life—the hideous dropping of the veil. There was an iciness, a sinking, a sickening of the heart—an unredeemed dreariness of thought which no goading of the imagination could torture into aught of the sublime. What was it—I paused to think—what was it that so unnerved me in the contemplation of the House of Usher? It was a mystery all insoluble; nor could I grapple with the shadowy fancies that crowded upon me as I pondered. I was forced to fall back upon the unsatisfactory conclusion, that while, beyond doubt, there *are* combinations of very simple natural objects which have the power of thus affecting us, still the analysis of the power lies among consider-ations beyond our depth. It was possible, I reflected, that a mere different arrangement of the particulars of the scene, of the details of the picture, would be sufficient to modify, or perhaps to annihilate its capacity for sorrowful impression; and, acting upon this idea, I reined my horse to the precipitous brink of a black and lurid tarn that lay in unruffled lustre by the dwelling, and gazed down—but with a shudder more thrilling than before—upon the remodelled and inverted images of the grey sedge, and the ghastly tree-stems, and the vacant and eye-like windows.

from 'The Fall of the House of Usher', *Tales of Mystery and Imagination* by Edgar Allan Poe

A broadcasting studio would, one might think, be the last place where one might meet a ghost. Not so, for the studios of BBC Radio Sheffield, built over a hundred years ago for a prominent citizen of the city, have a history which is beyond explanation, for amongst the modern, sophisticated equipment and the non-stop working atmosphere of today, something or somebody lingers.

I am indebted to Ralph Robinson, senior producer of BBC Radio Sheffield for allowing me to quote his article in the *Radio Sheffield Magazine*.

Says Ralph, 'It is one of the standing jokes of the station that the ghost may be somebody who was separated from a visiting party and expired whilst trying to find the way out.'

The building in Westbourne Road has a pleasant, rambling quality that can flummox many a first-time visitor. By day it can be eerie enough, but at night, with the wind rustling through the trees and the occasional owl hooting eerily in the branches, Ralph says, 'It can make Dracula's castle look like a Wendy House.'

Whoever or whatever the ghost might be, it is not a malevolent presence. Two people have claimed to have seen something, whilst others have heard it or sensed it. One young lady, who lives in Derbyshire, spent a late evening in Sheffield and had to get up very early in the morning to do an early shift at the studios. Instead of going home, she bedded down at the radio station but an hour later she got up and drove home because she felt she was not alone.

Ralph himself says that he has walked out three times late at night: once because strange things were happening to signal lights on electronic equipment and twice because he felt he was being watched.

A freelance reporter, Richard Hemmingway, was entirely on his own in the newsroom when he heard the front door open and footsteps go through the hall and up the stairs. He went to see who it was and found himself alone. Later he heard lights being switched on and off.

Not only is the presence felt late at night. One Sunday afternoon, engineer Peter Mason noticed that a recorded programme which was being broadcast had become barely audible. He hurried to the studio and found that a volume control knob on the main control panel had been turned down. No one had been in the studio and when he tried to reproduce the fault, he failed.

from *Ghosts and Yorkshire Legends* by Terence Whitaker

Encounters

THE GLIMPSE

She sped through the door
And, following in haste,
And stirred to the core,
I entered hot-faced;
But I could not find her,
No sign was behind her.
'Where is she?' I said:
— 'Who?' they asked that sat there;
'Not a soul's come in sight.'
— 'A maid with red hair.'
— 'Ah.' They paled. 'She is dead.
People see her at night,
But you are the first
On whom she has burst
In the keen common light.'

It was ages ago,
When I was quite strong:
I have waited since, — O,
I have waited so long!
— Yea, I set me to own
The house, where now lone
I dwell in void rooms
Booming hollow as tombs!
But I never come near her,
Though nightly I hear her.
And my cheek has grown thin
And my hair has grown gray
With this waiting therein;
But she still keeps away!

THOMAS HARDY

1 Read the poem carefully. Work with a partner. One of you
is the old man who has been waiting so long to see the ghostly
red-haired girl a second time. Your partner is the ghost, who at
long last visits him again. This time she speaks. Will she
explain her appearances? What kind of message does she have
for him? What is he hoping for from this ghostly meeting?

He must have slept soundly for an hour or more, when a sudden clatter shook him up in a most unwelcome manner. In a moment he realized what had happened: his carefully-constructed screen had given way, and a very bright frosty moon was shining directly on his face. This was highly annoying. Could he possibly get up and reconstruct the screen? or could he manage to sleep if he did not?

For some minutes he lay and pondered over the possibilities: then he turned over sharply, and with his eyes open lay breathlessly listening. There had been a movement, he was sure, in the empty bed on the opposite side of the room. Tomorrow he would have it moved, for there must be rats or something playing about in it. It was quiet now. No! the commotion began again. There was a rustling and shaking: surely more than any rat could cause.

I can figure to myself something of the Professor's bewilderment and horror, for I have in a dream thirty years back seen the same thing happen; but the reader will hardly, perhaps, imagine how dreadful it was to him to see a figure suddenly sit up in what he had known was an empty bed. He was out of his own bed in one bound, and made a dash towards the window, where lay his only weapon, the stick with which he had propped his screen. This was, as it turned out, the worst thing he could have done, because the personage in the empty bed, with a sudden smooth motion, slipped from the bed and took up a position, with outspread arms, between the two beds, and in front of the door. Parkins watched it in a horrid perplexity. Somehow the idea of getting past it and escaping through the door was intolerable to him; he could not have borne—he didn't know why—to touch it; and as for its touching him, he would sooner dash himself through the window than have that happen. It stood for the moment in a band of dark shadow, and he had not seen what its face was like. Now it began to move, in a stooping posture, and all at once the spectator realized, with some horror and some relief, that it must be blind, for it seemed to feel about with its muffled arms in a groping and random fashion. Turning half away from him, it became suddenly conscious of the bed he had just left, and darted towards it, and bent and felt over the pillows in a way which made Parkins shudder as he had never in his life thought it possible. In a very few moments it seemed to know that the bed was empty, and then, moving forward into the area of light and facing the window, it showed for the first time what manner of thing it was.

Parkins, who very much dislikes being questioned about it, did once describe something of it in my hearing, and I gathered that what he chiefly remembers about it is a horrible, an intensely horrible, face *of crumpled linen*. What expression he read upon it he could not or would not tell, but that the fear of it went nigh to maddening him is certain.

But he was not at leisure to watch it for long. With formidable quickness it moved into the middle of the room, and, as it groped and waved, one corner of its draperies swept across Parkins's face. He could not, though he knew how perilous a sound was — he could not keep back a cry of disgust, and this gave the searcher an instant clue. It leapt towards him upon the instant, and the next moment he was halfway through the window backwards, uttering cry upon cry at the utmost pitch of his voice, and the linen face was thrust close into his own. At this, almost the last possible second, deliverance came, as you will have guessed: the Colonel burst the door open, and was just in time to see the dreadful group at the window. When he reached the figures only one was left. Parkins sank forward into the room in a faint, and before him on the floor lay a tumbled heap of bed-clothes.

from 'Oh Whistle and I'll Come to You', *Ghost Stories of an Antiquary*

2 The Professor is very deeply affected by the fearful thing he encounters in his bedroom.

Work with a partner. One of you is the Professor, the other is a close friend of his or perhaps a medical person. Can you help the Professor to come to terms with what has happened? Can you get him to describe what he has seen? What steps can you take to prevent the thing from returning to haunt the Professor?

WHO'S THAT?

Who's that
stopping at
my door in the
dark, deep
in the dead of the moonless night?

Who's
that in the quiet
blackness,
darker than dark?

Who
turns the han-
dle of my door, who
turns the old brass hand-
le of
my door with never a sound, the handle
that always
creaks and rattles and
squeaks but
now
turns
without a sound, slowly
slowly
      slowly
           round?

Who's that moving through the floor
as if it were a lake, an open door? Who
is it who passes through
what can never be passed through,
who passes through
the rocking-chair
without rocking it,
who passes through
the table without knocking it, who
walks out of the cupboard without unlocking it?
Who's that? Who plays with my toys
with no noise, no
noise?

Who's that? Who is it
silent and silver
as things in mirrors, who's
as slow as feathers,
shy as the shivers,
light as a fly?

Who's that who's that
as close as
close as a hug, a kiss —

Who's THIS?

JAMES KIRKUP

3 Work in a small group. Using movement and sound, but no words, can you create a scene which will capture the feeling of the poem 'Who's That?' Share your scenes with the rest of the class.

Special Powers

THE KNOWLEDGEABLE CHILD

I always see,—I don't know why,—
If any person's going to die.

That's why nobody talks to me.
There was a man who came to tea,

And when I saw that he would die
I went to him and said 'Good-bye,

'I shall not see you any more.'
He died that evening. Then, next door,

They had a little girl: she died
Nearly as quick, and Mummy cried

And cried, and ever since that day
She's made me promise not to say.

But folks are still afraid of me,
And, where they've children, nobody

Will let me next or nigh to them
For fear I'll say good-bye to them.

LEONARD ALFRED GEORGE STRONG

The family of this child with special powers may be made to feel like outsiders in their community, and the child is probably very lonely.

1 Work in a small group. One of you is the parent of the knowledgeable child. The others are neighbours who want the family to move away because they are afraid of what may happen. What can the parents say? Do the neighbours succeed in their request?

2   In the play, Oliver seems to have special powers of understanding.

Invent a scene in which Oliver's special powers are used at school, or among his friends. How will his classmates feel about him?

3   Oliver found a baby's rattle and part of a silk shawl in the Morrissey shelter. Imagine that you have found something linked with the past — the ring from the finger of a missing girl, the spectacles of a murdered man. What effect do these objects have when you bring them home? Consider the possibilites — a haunting, possession, bad dreams. Write a short story in which you recount what effect they have on your life.

4   Imagine that you are a ghost. Perhaps you haunt some very unexpected place — the school lab., a bus shelter, a disco, the youth club. Describe one night of your hauntings, and the effect you have on the people who see you.

5   Write a short story entitled:
'The ghost on the telephone', 'The fatal key' or 'Blood will have blood'.

LAND, FOOD, FAMINE

The Dust Bowl

In the America of the 1930s an area including the states of
Oklahoma, Kansas, Utah and Colorado became known as the
Dust Bowl. The poor tenant farmers were faced with eviction
from their land, just as, nearly a century earlier, Irish peasants
had been evicted from their land and homes. The causes of this
crisis, however, were different. The land in the Dust Bowl
states had become degraded — the poor soil had been
overfarmed during a period of many years and had lost its
ability to retain moisture. The dusty topsoil was prey to winds
which blew it away. Each year the crops of the tenant farmers
were poorer — each year the land was less able to support their
corn. It could still grow cotton, but for this machines and much
larger tracts of land offered the most efficient return on the
investment. There was no place in the scheme for the share-
croppers. As in the Irish Famine, evictions were common. The
following extract is taken from John Steinbeck's novel, *The
Grapes of Wrath*.

The owners of the land came on to the land, or more often a
spokesman for the owners came. They came in closed cars, and
they felt the dry earth with their fingers, and sometimes they
drove big earth augers into the ground for soil tests. The
tenants, from their sun-beaten dooryards, watched uneasily
when the closed cars drove along the fields. And at last the
owner men drove into the dooryards and sat in their cars to talk
out of the windows. The tenant men stood beside the cars for a
while, and then squatted on their hams and found sticks with
which to mark the dust.

In the open doors the women stood looking out, and behind
them the children — corn-headed children, with wide eyes, one
bare foot on top of the other bare foot, and the toes working. The
women and the children watched their men talking to the owner

men. They were silent.

Some of the owner men were kind because they hated what they had to do, and some of them were angry because they hated to be cruel, and some of them were cold because they had long ago found that one could not be an owner unless one were cold. And all of them were caught in something larger than themselves. Some of them hated the mathematics that drove them, and some were afraid, and some worshipped the mathematics because it provided a refuge from thought and from feeling. If a bank or a finance company owned the land, the owner man said: The Bank — or the Company — needs — wants — insists — must have — as though the Bank or the Company were a monster, with thought and feeling, which had ensnared them. These last would take no responsibility for the banks or the companies because they were men and slaves, while the banks were machines and masters all at the same time. Some of the owner men were a little proud to be slaves to such cold and powerful masters. The owner men sat in the cars and explained. You know the land is poor. You've scrabbed at it long enough, God knows.

The squatting tenant men nodded and wondered and drew figures in the dust, and yes, they knew, God knows. If the dust only wouldn't fly. If the top would only stay on the soil, it might not be so bad.

The owner men went on leading to their point: You know the land's getting poorer. You know what cotton does to the land: robs it, sucks all the blood out of it.

The squatters nodded — they knew, God knew. If they could

Dust Bowl district in Dalhart, Texas, 1938

only rotate the crops they might pump blood back into the land.

Well, it's too late. And the owner men explained the workings and the thinkings of the monster that was stronger than they were. A man can hold land if he can just eat and pay taxes: he can do that.

Yes, he can do that until his crops fail one day and he has to borrow money from the bank.

But — you see, a bank or a company can't do that, because those creatures don't breathe air, don't eat side-meat. They breathe profits; they eat the interest on money. If they don't get it, they die the way you die without air, without side-meat. It is a sad thing, but it is so. It is just so.

The squatting men raised their eyes to understand. Can't we just hang on? Maybe the next year will be a good year. God knows how much cotton next year. And with all the wars — God knows what price cotton will bring. Don't they make explosives out of cotton? And uniforms? Get enough wars and cotton'll hit the ceiling. Next year, maybe. They looked up questioningly.

We can't depend on it. The bank — the monster has to have profits all the time. It can't wait. It'll die. No, taxes go on. When the monster stops growing, it dies. It can't stay one size.

Soft fingers began to tap the sill of the car window, and hard fingers tightened on the restless drawing sticks. In the doorways of the sun-beaten tenant houses women sighed and then shifted feet so that the one that had been down was now on top, and the toes working. Dogs came sniffing near the owner cars and wetted on all four tyres one after another. And chickens lay in the sunny dust and fluffed their feathers to get the cleansing dust down to the skin. In the little styes the pigs grunted inquiringly over the muddy remnants of the slops.

The squatting men looked down again. What do you want us to do? We can't take less share of the crop — we're half-starved now. The kids are hungry all the time. We got no clothes, torn an' ragged. If all the neighbours weren't the same, we'd be ashamed to go to meeting.

And at last the owner men came to the point. The tenant system won't work any more. One man on a tractor can take the place of twelve or fourteen families. Pay him a wage and take all the crop. We have to do it. We don't like to do it. But the monster's sick. Something's happened to the monster.

But you'll kill the land with cotton.

We know. We've got to take cotton quick before the land dies. Then we'll sell the land. Lots of families in the East would like to own a piece of land.

The tenant men looked up alarmed. But what'll happen to us? How'll we eat?

You'll have to get off the land. The ploughs'll go through the door-yard.

A family leave their farm near Fort Gibson in Muskogee County, Oklahoma, 1939

And now the squatting men stood up angrily. Grampa took up the land, and he had to kill the Indians and drive them away. And Pa was born here, and he killed weeds and snakes. Then a bad year came and he had to borrow a little money. An' we was born here. There in the door — our children born here. And Pa had to borrow money. The bank owned the land then, but we stayed and we got a little bit of what we raised.

We know that — all that. It's not us, it's the bank. A bank isn't like a man. Or an owner with fifty thousand acres, he isn't like a man either. That's the monster.

Sure, cried the tenant men, but it's our land. We measured it and broke it up. We were born on it, and we got killed on it, died on it. Even if it's no good, it's still ours. That's what makes it ours — being born on it, working it, dying on it. That makes ownership, not a paper with numbers on it.

We're sorry. It's not us. It's the monster. The bank isn't like a man.

Yes, but the bank is only made of men.

No, you're wrong there — quite wrong there. The bank is something else than men. It happens that every man in a bank hates what the bank does, and yet the bank does it. The bank is something more than men, I tell you. It's the monster. Men made it, but they can't control it.

The tenants cried: Grampa killed Indians, Pa killed snakes for the land. Maybe we can kill banks — they're worse than Indians and snakes. Maybe we got to fight to keep our land, like Pa and Grampa did.

And now the owner men grew angry. You'll have to go.

But it's ours, the tenant men cried. We. . .

No. The bank, the monster owns it. You'll have to go.

We'll get our guns, like Grampa when the Indians came. What then?

Well — first the sheriff, and then the troops. You'll be stealing if you try to stay, you'll be murderers if you kill to stay. The monster isn't men, but it can make men do what it wants.

But if we go, where'll we go? How'll we go? We got no money.

We're sorry, said the owner men. The bank, the fifty-thousand-acre owner can't be responsible. You're on land that isn't yours. Once over the line maybe you can pick cotton in the fall. Maybe you can go on relief. Why don't you go on west to California? There's work there, and it never gets cold. Why, you can reach out anywhere and pick an orange. Why, there's always some kind of crop to work in. Why don't you go there? And the owner men started their cars and rolled away.

The tenant men squatted down on their hams again to mark the dust with a stick, to figure, to wonder. Their sun-burned faces were dark, and their sun-whipped eyes were light. The women moved cautiously out of the doorways towards their men, and the children crept behind the women, cautiously, ready to run. The bigger boys squatted beside their fathers, because that made them men. After a time the women asked: What did they want?

And the men looked up for a second, and the smoulder of pain was in their eyes. We got to set off. A tractor and a super-intendent. Like factories.

Where'll we go? the women asked.

We don't know. We don't know.

---

1 Look again at the passage where the owners come to announce their plans to the tenants. Produce a script from this material. Sometimes you will have to write your own lines, sometimes you can use the exact words from the novel. You must make sure that your words and Steinbeck's words match up, that they are in the same style and tone or your script will be uneven and unconvincing.

Alternatively, you could use a mixture of improvisation and voice-over narration to present these scenes. Mime and tableaux with narration could also be effective. In fact, you might try all these techniques in one performance. Which technique is most suited to the opening paragraph? Which is best for the section beginning 'The owner men went on leading to their point: You know the land's getting poorer.'? Experiment. Choose what works best.

Recent Famines

In October 1984 the news of the Ethiopian famine broke in the West. At that time things were so bad that someone died of starvation every twenty minutes. Three per hour.

In those first newsreels we saw interminable queues waiting to be fed. Some stood within the emergency centres' low walls, some waited outside. There was only enough food for those on the right side of the wall. No-one was climbing over. They were beyond hope, exhausted by hunger. In numb despair they stood in line on the wrong side of the wall. If someone fed them they would eat, if no food was offered they would die. They could do no more. With a terrible fatalism they stood on the wrong side of that wall and waited.

1   Write a piece called 'The Wrong Side of the Wall.' It may take any form — a personal account, a newspaper article, a poem or play. You could even take the idea one step further, and see the wall of the emergency aid centre as the divide between the rich countries we live in and the poverty of the developing world.

2   Imagine returning home after a long absence. There has been a drought, perhaps, and now there is famine. Is your home still standing or is it destroyed? Your family is not there. Working in a small group, improvise your return and subsequent search for them. You could set your play in any country using the background of the African famine, or in Britain after some terrible disaster, natural or manmade, has completely ended our current way of life.

3   Plan an advertising campaign to raise money for Ethiopia or another stricken area. Consider the different types of advertising. Remember to include the script of a speech to be broadcast on radio or TV. If you choose to write for television you should give some idea of what viewers will see while they hear the appeal. For example:

Camera	Script
Close up of face. Open shot to include whole figure and camp with refugees.	Today a child will die. Tomorrow a child will die, because here in the Sudan the crops have failed again.

AT THE FAO in Rome, officials display a considerable range of views about how future famines can be avoided. There are still those, like the Ethiopian who heads its African bureau, who talk about the need for a massive aid programme, massive concentrations of technology and an enormous (Western) task force to build railways, dams, roads and airports — 'hundreds of billions of dollars, that is the kind of thing we are talking about . . . that is the only way.'

Yet, though many of his colleagues are also convinced that large amounts of aid will be needed, his way was by no means the predominant tone. What it would take to cure famine, declared one senior planner, was just two words, political will: political will, that is to say, on the part of African governments to commit themselves to a policy of agricultural development for 20 years. Malawi was not a rich country, but it had done it and so could others.

'Unless that happens,' said David Norse, head of a team preparing a study on how Africa can get out of its present dilemma, 'nothing will change, no matter how much aid is poured in.'

He didn't believe aid should be cut off, but it should certainly be reoriented to promote self-help. Africa was full of self-help if only we encouraged it instead of killing it. If they themselves at the FAO received a cable asking for help, they felt they had to send some. More often, their reply ought to be: 'Sort it out yourself.'

Like some of his colleagues, his major doubt is whether African governments will actually start helping their farmers. 'If they get food aid, subsidised imports and have a politically active population in the cities,' said one, 'why should they raise the prices they give farmers? It is the 10 per cent who live in the cities who will continue to decide, not the 90 per cent who live God knows where.'

'These countries have accepted such fantastic amounts of foreign food in the form of wheat and rice,' said one of Norse's colleagues, 'that now the people in the cities don't want to eat domestic grains like millet and sorghum.' So, yes, food aid had actually made things harder for the local farmers.

Sunday Telegraph, 14 July 1985

Geldof ravages Europe's excesses

Fresh from his tour of famine stricken Africa, Mr Bob Geldof yesterday came to Strasbourg, world capital of gluttony, and took the European parliament by storm.

Before a massed audience of MEPs, reporters, parliamentary staff, fans, and infants, he savaged the Common Agricultural Policy ('the crowning idiocy'), EEC Bureaucracy ('this place needs a laxative'), and party bickering ('I'm pissed off about it'). It was a great success.

Commissioner Willy de Clercq tried in vain to smother the Geldof appeal with an interminable explanation of the complexities of food aid. The British Labour group tried in vain to explain why they boycotted a lunch (sandwiches only) with him. A French reporter tried in vain to question his knowledge of the CAP.

It was all swept aside by the unassailable logic and unstoppable passion of the Geldof line: people are starving to death there, and we have mountains of food here.

It was preposterous, an outrage, and made no economic and moral sense. How to get rid of the mountains? Give them away. How to mobilise European economic power? Launch a Marshall plan for Africa. How to respond to emergency needs? Set up a 10-man task force, free of red tape. He promised that unless parliament restored cuts made by national governments in next year's food aid budget, he would 'fuss, bluster, fume and rage and generally behave like a popstar.'

The Guardian, 24 October 1985

1 Why do some people feel that aid should be cut?

2 Are all of the government's reasons for cutting aid the same?

3 Compare the European Parliament's attitude to aid with the attitude shown by the English government during the Irish Famine.

Where has all the food gone?

Below is the cover of a pamphlet produced by Oxfam. Read the other extracts from the pamphlet which follow. These give some insights into the way world food production is organised. Make a list of the points which are being made, then write a paragraph which takes as its opening statement: 'Massive famine is inevitable by the year 2000 unless. . .'

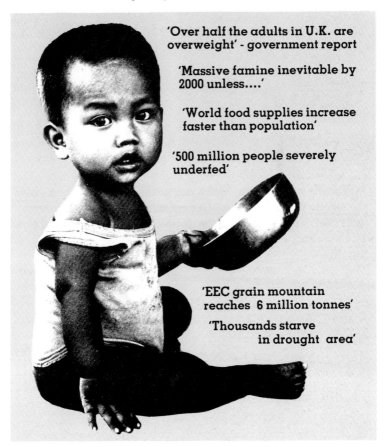

'Over half the adults in U.K. are overweight' - government report

'Massive famine inevitable by 2000 unless....'

'World food supplies increase faster than population'

'500 million people severely underfed'

'EEC grain mountain reaches 6 million tonnes'

'Thousands starve in drought area'

Most developing countries have little industry and therefore export agricultural products or minerals (copper, for instance). They desperately need to buy goods from other countries, yet they find it impossible to pay for everything they want out of their export earnings. Balancing the budget can be a problem for any government, but in developing countries where there are so many needs and so little to meet them with, the problems are enormous.

More than a third of all the grain grown in the world is used to feed animals. But in most countries meat is so expensive that the poor can rarely afford it. Raising cattle or sheep may make good sense where land is unsuitable for growing crops, but when animals have to be fed large amounts of food which could be eaten by people, meat production is very wasteful.

In the last century or so, wherever Europeans settled or traded, they encouraged people to sow crops that were wanted in Europe. So cash crops (i.e. crops for sale) replaced food crops in many areas.

Maybe it's too simple to blame one group of people: but it's also too simple to blame nature! Governments, companies and rich merchants all play their part in deciding the amount of food that is available and who will eat it. Here's an example:

In 1970 the world's granaries were overflowing with wheat. The price, therefore, was low, and farmers in the United States grumbled because they were not making as much money as they would have liked. The government decided to pay them not to plant. In 1972, 5 million acres were taken out of production — an amount equal to all the farmland in the UK. As luck would have it, drought hit 18 countries, including those in the Sahel, that very same year. The price of wheat shot up and millions suffered because they were too poor to buy it. But, of course, anyone who had wheat to sell did well. 'America's farm problem is not how to grow more food but how to grow less'.

(Nation's Business 1969)

But in times of famine, isn't food really short?

Let's look at an example: the Sahel famine, in which thousands of people and cattle died in 1972/73, in the countries bordering the Sahara Desert. The famine was caused by drought, we were told. But the fact is that these countries have lived with drought for hundreds of years. The nomads who live in the Sahara are expert at coping with such conditions.

There were many other reasons why they suffered so badly this time.

Nor was food really short. During the drought, exports actually increased. Ships bringing relief food to West Africa left loaded with peanuts, cotton, vegetables, and meat. Some farmers, therefore, could irrigate their land well enough to grow crops in spite of the drought. Over the years they had received a lot of help from companies, government, and international agencies to enable them to do so.

In the meantime, the production of crops for local people to eat — maize, millet, and sorghum — fell. (And they are still falling in some areas.) Yet, some experts say there would still have been enough to go round if food had been shared out properly.

High prices here in Britain don't necessarily mean a high income for those people in other countries who grow our food.

91

ACTIVITIES MAPPING

English Framework Objectives (Year 7/8/9)

Page Number		Learning Objectives (Year 7/8/9)			
	Word (W) & Sentence (S) Level	Text Level			Speaking & Listening
		Reading	Writing		
57–9					(7) 13, 15, 16, 17, 19 (8) 3, 14, 15, 16 (9) 10, 11, 12, 14
59	(7) S14, S15 (8) W12, S12 (9) S3	(7) 4, 7, 8	(7) 2, 6, 7, 8, 10, 14 (8) 5, 6, 7, 10		
60	(7) S13, S14, S15 (8) S2, S9, S12 (9) S3	(7) 4, 7, 8	(7) 2, 6, 7, 8, 10, 14 (8) 5, 6, 7, 10, 12		
63		(7) 6, 8	(7) 6, 8, 9, 14 (8) 6, 7		(7) 12, 13, 15, 16, 17, 19 (8) 10, 11, 14, 15, 16 (9) 12, 14
70–1					(7) 13, 15, 16, 17, 19 (8) 14, 15, 16 (9) 12, 14

72	(7) S13, S14, S15 (8) S2, S9, S12 (9) S3	(7) 4, 7, 8	(7) 6, 7, 8, 10, 14 (8) 5, 6, 7, 10, 12	
73	(8) W11	(7) 14 (8) 10	(7) 4	(7) 2, 11, 12, 13, 15, 16, 17 (8) 14, 15, 16 (9) 12, 14
76		(7) 6, 8		(7) 13, 14, 15, 16, 17, 18 (8) 14, 15, 16 (9) 12, 14
78				(7) 13, 15, 16, 17, 18 (8) 14, 15, 16 (9) 12, 14
80				(7) 13, 15, 16, 17 (8) 14, 15, 16 (9) 12, 14
81			(7) 5, 6, 7, 8 (8) 5, 6, 7 (9) 5	(7) 13, 15, 16, 17 (8) 14, 15, 16 (9) 12, 14
86			(7) 9	(7) 13, 15, 16, 17 (8) 14, 15, 16 (9) 12, 14
87	(8) S9		(7) 6, 7, 8, 14 (8) 5, 6, 7 (9) 13	(7) 13, 15, 16, 17 (8) 14, 15, 16 (9) 12, 14
89		(7) 2, 4, 7, 8 (8) 1, 12, 13	(7) 11, 12, 16 (8) 17	

Collins | Plays Plus

Other titles in the **Collins** Plays Plus and
Plays Plus Classics series that you might enjoy:

The Tulip Touch

ANNE FINE

A stunning adaptation by the author of
the best-selling novel featuring the story
of a disturbed teenager.
Themes: Juvenile crime; growing up and
friendship
Cast: 22 characters (plus extras)

ISBN 0 00 713086 4

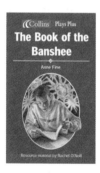

The Book of the Banshee

ANNE FINE

Adapted by Anne Fine from her popular
novel, this is the story of teenage rebellion
and its effects on a family.
Themes: Gender roles; family; growing up;
pacifism and rebellion
Cast: 6 characters

ISBN 0 00 330310 1

Flour Babies

ANNE FINE

The amusing and moving adaptation of
the novel exploring one boy's attempt to
come to terms with his absent father
through a school project on parenting.
Themes: Parenting; family
Cast: 19 characters

ISBN 0 00 330312 8

The Granny Project

ANNE FINE

When Ivan finds himself responsible for looking after his grandmother single-handedly he finds he has more than he had bargained for. The play is a humorous take on family roles and sensitively explores the issue of ageism.

Themes: Ageism; family roles; parenting
Cast: 7 characters

ISBN 0 00 330234 2

Dear Nobody

BERLIE DOHERTY

Adapted from the award-winning book, this play examines how two teenagers cope with an unplanned pregnancy.

Themes: Teenage pregnancy; relationships; growing up
Cast: 16 characters

ISBN 0 00 320004 3

Mean to be Free

JOANNA HALPERT KRAUS

Set in America's deep south in the 19th century, this is the true story of Harriet Tubman, an ex-slave, who led slaves to freedom in Canada.

Themes: Slavery; freedom
Cast: 15 characters

ISBN 0 00 330240 7

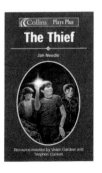

The Thief

JAN NEEDLE

Focusing on a boy falsely accused of stealing, *The Thief* is a stimulating school-based drama.

Themes: Youth crime; self-deception; prejudice
Cast: 20 characters

ISBN 0 00 330237 7

The Bully

JAN NEEDLE

An adaptation of the best-selling novel that explores the unsentimental and realistic aspects of bullying and its impact in schools.
Themes: Bullying
Cast: 12 characters (plus extras)

ISBN 0 00 330227 X

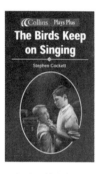

The Birds Keep on Singing

STEPHEN COCKETT

The story of three evacuees billeted with two sisters during World War II. As the adults struggle to cope, the children come to a truce of their own.
Themes: War; relationships
Cast: 11 characters

ISBN 0 00 330315 2

In Holland Stands a House

SUE SAUNDERS

Based on the plight of Anne Frank who, with her family, went into hiding during the Nazi occupation. Drawing on her diary, the play skilfully interweaves domestic scenes from the annexe with wider events happening in Europe.
Themes: The Holocaust; racism; family; relationships
Cast: 11 characters (plus chorus)

ISBN 0 00 330242 3

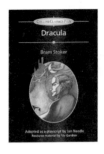

Dracula

BRAM STOKER
(Adapted by Jan Needle)

A blood-sucking count who lives in a coffin – is this the vision of a madman, or a terrible truth? This is a dark dramatisation of Stoker's classic horror story.

Themes: Gender roles; death
Cast: 14 characters

ISBN 0 00 330224 5

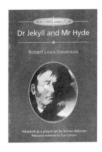

Dr Jekyll and Mr Hyde

ROBERT LOUIS STEVENSON
(Adapted by Simon Adorian)

Presented in the form of a TV documentary involving expert witnesses trying to get to the bottom of the mystery surrounding Dr Jekyll and Mr Hyde, this dramatisation of Stevenson's classic tale is ideal for use in schools.

Themes: Drugs; transformation; mental illness; the media
Cast: 19 characters (plus chorus)

ISBN 0 00 323078 3